BAD

&

BOUJEE

AN URBAN LOVE TALE BY

SASHA DAVENPORT

www.jadedpublications.com

TO BE NOTIFIED OF NEW RELEASES, CONTESTS, GIVEAWAYS,

AND BOOK SIGNINGS IN YOUR AREA, TEXT **BOOKS** TO **44144**

This novel is a work of fiction. Any reference to real people, events, establishments, or locales is intended only to give the fiction a sense of reality and authenticity. Other names, characters, and incidents occurring in the work are either the product of the author's imagination or are used fictitiously, as are those fictionalized events and events that involve real persons. Any character that happens to share the name of a person who is any acquaintance of the author, past or present, is purely coincidental and is in no way intended to be an actual account involving that person.

Copyright © 2016

1

ALAÏA

Contemporary music thumped through the speakers of *Flight*, a newly opened outdoor nightclub in West Hollywood that was known for attracting movie stars, athletes, music artists, and professionals from all walks of life. On a Friday evening, the place was jam-packed, with me and my girls shuffling through the crowds of wealthy powerhouses to be seen—though it wasn't hard for a couple of bad bitches like us.

Dressed in designer wear from our head to our thousand dollar shoes, we easily were mistaken as *The Real Housewives of Beverly Hills*. Unfortunately, all three of our asses were single, which led us to the enthralls of the vibrant and vigorous LA nightlife. Maybe one of us would be lucky enough to snag a baller or at least a nigga on our echelon, because Lord knows as a successful black woman in America, that challenge could be quite difficult—especially when you were as bougie as us.

As we navigated through the crowd of club-goers, I briefly locked gazes with a tall, suited, caramel brotha with poise and an elegant flare about himself. His handsome face, perfectly cut features, muscles, and tall height were all overwhelming for a human being. The man was fine as shit but he didn't look like he had enough racks to fuck with me.

You see, living in Hollywood meant that you had to be able to spot the real from the fake. Broke and opportunistic people loved mingling with the upper echelons of the hierarchical system. Not only did it make them look good, but it gave them an opportunity to finesse their way into our social circle for their own personal gain. But that was Hollywood for you, and believe me, I was the last bitch a mothafucka would get over on.

Halfway to the bar, Miracle was stopped by a sexy Persian guy. "Hey, baby. You got a little time to spend with me tonight. I won't take too much of your time. I only need a little," he promised. "What's your name, baby?"

"Miracle."

He smiled. "And why do they call you that?"

"Because I make dreams come true," she said persuasively.

"How can I be a part of that dream?"

"I don't invest my time in nothing less than seven-figure niggas."

With a defeated look, he walked off, knowing damn well the bar she'd set was too high for him. While Miracle and Chloè laughed at his humiliation, I peered over my shoulder to see if the nigga was still looking at me. He was.

I don't know why the fuck he's staring at me like that. I ain't got shit for his ass. Not even an autograph.

I laughed under my breath cynically at the very thought of him acting like a groupie. Usually, when people spotted me, that was their automatic reaction. Speaking of which, a woman gleefully waved in my direction after recognizing who I was. Before I could tell her that I wasn't taking any pictures, she rushed over, damn near knocking my best friend/publicist out of the way.

"Oh my God, Alaïa Westbrook!" she exclaimed, bubbling with excitement. "I can't believe it's really you! You're even more beautiful in person! Oh my God! Can we please take a picture together? My sister is not gonna believe this! She's such a big fan of yours too!"

My home girl Miracle stepped up to politely turn her down, but I quickly intervened, telling her that I would make a one-time exception. Besides, I was in a good mood—and the poor girl was beyond star-struck. So much so, that she'd probably kill herself if I turned her away; that's how thrilled she was to see me. Then again, I had that effect on just about everyone.

Flipping my long, bone straight hair over my shoulder, I leaned down so that I was level with her short frame and posed for a selfie. After she anxiously uploaded it to Snapchat, she thanked me again and sauntered off with the joy of someone who'd just hit the Mega Millions.

For some strange reason, my eyes wandered over towards the man who was ogling me earlier. Apart of me hoped he'd witnessed the interaction with my fan so that I could silently gloat in triumph.

Much to my dismay, he had his back turned to me and was now conversing with a middle-aged white couple. *Damn him. Who told him it was okay to stop admiring me*, I sulked mentally. Just because I wasn't entertaining his lustful stares didn't mean that I didn't enjoy the attention.

"I can't believe this place is this crowded!" I yelled over the music, dismissing the man from my thoughts. I was stunning that evening in a form-fitting beige skirt. The red, long sleeve blouse shirt I wore had a plunging neckline that showed off my perfect cleavage. I'd never actually gone under the knife, but gossip blogs were always writing articles that argued otherwise. As a matter of fact, they were *always* spreading lies about me but it was something that inevitably came with the territory of being a rising Hollywood actress.

Flipping my hair over my shoulder, I looked over in the direction of my secret admirer to see if he'd returned to gawking at me. It was funny how just a few seconds ago, I'd written the nigga off, but I guess since he was cute or whatever I kinda craved his attention and approval. Even though I was filthy rich and beautiful, I was still insecure to some extent.

No one knew that about me. Not even my BFFs.

I mean, what woman who looked like me would carry around her insecurities like luggage? On the outside, I was practically perfect with my statuesque height, smooth honey-colored skin, high cheekbones, hazel eyes, and piercing dimples. I was known for being the porcelain poster child of good looks and had even snagged a few endorsements with cosmetic lines and shampoo brands, which featured me on billboards throughout the city. I was known as the it-girl. There were even women who'd undergone surgery just to resemble me. But regardless of all that, I was still secretly precarious enough to long for the approval of a complete stranger.

Why isn't he looking at me anymore, I thought wistfully.

The white couple had wandered off somewhere and now he was alone, nursing a shot of whatever was in his cup.

"I can believe it. Folks are always scrambling to be at the hottest, newest establishments," Miracle explained. "Even if they're crammed like a can of sardines, they just have to make their presence be known." She laughed. "That's Hollywood for you."

Miracle was my publicist and best friend. We attended the same high school and film school. Sad to say, her career as an actress never quite took off like mine—but she devoted herself to keeping me relevant and successful, always striving to see me win. Because of that, she was like family to me. Miracle never came off as jealous or spiteful. She was genuine, kind-hearted, and good-natured. Perhaps even too good for someone like me, but I cherished our friendship and the fact that she was one of the realest people I knew.

Standing at a mere 5"1, Miracle's even-toned skin was the color of milk chocolate, and she wore her long wavy hair gray with blue undertones. She was incredibly pretty with both an urban and wholesome appeal, and the rich white boys and Armenians loved her.

Once we finally made it to the bar, Chloè was the first one to order per usual. "Let me get a double shot of Avion," she said, placing her Chanel bag on the countertop.

At twenty-six, she was the oldest of our trio and a stone cold alcoholic due to mommy issues. Apparently, all throughout her life, her mom had pimped her out to Hollywood A-listers, rappers, and anyone that would pay to have the biracial bombshell on their arm to make them look good. Half-black, half-Italian, Chloè was the epitome of beauty with her smooth, butterscotch skin, delicate facial features, and modelesque figure. Men and women alike desired her, but she only had time for the elite.

Chloè was a high-profile escort that only dated the rich and famous. She refused to turn a trick less than $10,000. And like me, she too had plundering self-esteem issues that pushed her to the point of bleaching her skin and undergoing multiple surgeries to chase perfection.

She also attended the same film school as me and Miracle, but she dropped out, citing she would make more money turning tricks. Though that's what she claimed, I was sure her mother played a huge role in her decision. To this very day, she was still calling all the shots in her daughter's life like she was her fucking manager. Oftentimes, Miracle and I would teasingly call her a "momager"—which was just a fancy term for a pimp. I didn't like the shit at all but to each his own. At the end of the day, we were all just trying to get it how we lived. Some definitely more than others.

"What are ya'll having?" Chloè asked, preparing to pay for our drinks.

"I'll take my usual. A shot of Hennessey," Miracle said.

Before I could respond, I suddenly caught my admirer staring in my direction again. Inflated with arrogance, I smiled and tucked my hair behind my ear.

Without warning, he slowly made his way over towards me.

Oh, God. Here he comes, I thought to myself. *Now I'm gonna have to find a way to turn his fine ass down easy.*

He was just about to open his mouth to greet me when I quickly cut him off. "Look, nigga, I know the game you're finna run and ain't nobody playing yo bullshit today."

He looked confused by my bold assertion, but I decided to continue anyway.

"I know what you're thinking. You see a bad bitch with her friends and assume she's single and desperate. And I can assure you the latter of which, I am certainly not! You see, I've got standards. Standards that you obviously fail to meet," I said, looking at his non-designer loafers. "So get the fuck out my face 'cuz you don't stand a chance getting my mothafucking number."

Instead of being offended, he gave me a charming smile and handed me a napkin. "Well, at least get rid of that shit on your shoulder. It's unbecoming."

At first, I assumed he was hitting me with some catchy apothegm until I looked over and noticed a beetle crawling on my shirt. "*EEEEEEKKKKKK!*"

Smacking the little bugger off me, I looked up to scold him and noticed that he was gone, just like that. I felt like a fucking fool after realizing his only reason for approaching me was to tell me that there was a bug on me.

Asshole.

With bitterness coursing through my veins, I crushed the beetle with the heel of my Giuseppes, wishing it was his pride instead of mine that was now wounded.

"Bitch, you were taking too long to order, so I got you a double shot of Henny," Chloè said, handing me the glass.

I frowned my face up in disgust. "You know I hate dark liquor."

"Ho, you gon' like it tonight," she insisted, pushing the shot glass in my hands.

Chloè was the only person who talked to and treated me like I wasn't a famous celebrity, and I loved her for that shit. When you were rich and famous, you were always surrounded by people kissing your ass and lying to you to stay on your good side, but I never got that treatment from my girls. They never kissed up to me or fed me bullshit for the sake of remaining friends. They kept it real with me 24/7. Maybe even a little *too* real at times.

"And who the hell was that you were just talking to?" Miracle asked curiously. "He was finer than a dog's hair split three ways. I know you ain't just curve his cute ass."

"I knooooow. He's sexy as shit, ain't he," the bartender chimed in. "And filthy fucking rich too. He owns this nightclub and a few other ones throughout Los Angeles."

Now I felt like an even bigger fool after hearing that shit. "He—he's the owner?" I repeated, cheeks flushing in embarrassment. I'd talked to him so recklessly not knowing that I was a guest in *his* establishment. "I—I had no idea."

The bartender chuckled. "Most people don't. He's real low-key, likes to fly under the radar to avoid unwanted attention. Every so often, he'll make a cameo to see how business is going."

"But is he single?" Chloè butted in. "That's the real question!"

"He's the target of a lot of romance speculation. But I believe he's single. I mean, it's not like I ever see him with other women."

"Well…is he…" Miracle's voice trailed off. She didn't want to mouth off that he could possibly be gay. After all, we were in West Hollywood.

"Nah. I doubt it. Like I said, he's just a low-key type of brother. Always moving in silence and solitude. No one really knows much about his personal life. He likes to keep to himself."

"*Mmm.* My type of brotha," Chloè said, licking her filler-injected lips. They reminded me of Angelina Jolie's famous soup-coolers. "I like my niggas discreet."

As Miracle, Chloè, and the bartender swooned over the mysterious club owner, I couldn't help but stand there speechless and dumbfounded. I'd treated the man like shit and now I felt awful about it.

I was always bitching about how hard it was to find a man on my level. Now that I finally came across the perfect suitor, I ran his ass away with arrogance and materialistic pride.

Dammit, Alaïa! Way to fucking go!

As if my night could get any worse, things really took a turn when my ex-boyfriend Zane showed up with his new bitch Tika, latched onto his arm like an infant to a tit. Ugh! *Why the fuck is his black ass here? And tonight, of all nights?*

Los Angeles was a big city. The odds of randomly bumping into someone you didn't want to were slim, and yet there he was, swaggering through the nightclub like he owned the bitch. Just the sight of him made my ass itch, and I was tempted to slap the smug ass grin off of his girl's face.

"Bitch, is that Z?!" Chloè asked, suspended in disbelief. Miracle's head whipped in his direction. She was just as shocked as us to see him standing there in the flesh. "What the fuck is he doing here?"

The club lit up as cameramen rushed to snap photos of Zane and Tika. He was a big-time producer who collaborated with a plethora of famous artists, including The Game, YG, Nipsey Hussle, and Kid Ink. He was a cocky mothafucka who wore his arrogance on his sleeve, and all the bitches in LA loved him. Draped in chains and designer from his head down to his feet, he had the swagger of a mob boss. But what the fans and media didn't know was that Zane truly was the plug behind the scenes. He supplied nothing but A-listers and wealthy businessmen, so his revenue far exceeded that of a music producer's. The nigga was filthy fucking rich and he was doing major things in the entertainment industry.

It could've easily been me that was latched onto his arm, but I left his no good, abusive ass 2 years ago, and ironically, that's when my career took off. I started getting deals left and right, and all sorts of doors began to open for me. I was showered in endless opportunities the second I left his trifling ass alone. They say the best way to move forward is to let go of the people holding you back. That had never been more apparent to me after wiping my hands clean of Zane.

"Did you snap or post to your IG?" Chloè asked.

"No, I—" All of a sudden, it hit me. The chick I took a photo with earlier posted the selfie, therefore giving away my location. "I didn't, but I know who did."

"That little bitch! See, I told you that's why you shouldn't take pictures with groupies!" Miracle complained. "There could be some deranged nigga out there obsessing over you."

"I'm sure there's plenty niggas out there obsessing over her," Chloè laughed.

"My point is, someone could show up to where you are, put a gun to your head and blow your mothafucking brains out! Let's just be thankful that someone is your ex and not a deranged ass lunatic."

"Ok, stop being overdramatic bitch. You're her publicist, not her parent," Chloè snickered. She and Miracle were forever going at it over me.

Looking back in Zane's direction, I rolled my eyes in utter disgust. *So, I'm guessing he showed up with that bitch to make me jealous.* Little did he know, that little tactic had no effect on me whatsoever. Any feelings I had for his arrogant ass were dead and gone.

As if sensing our prying eyes, Zane looked my way and grinned mischievously. He was just as messy as I'd always known him to be, flaunting his new chick like she was his prize, hoping that would get a rise out of me.

Shit, he's coming this way!

"Wus good Chloè, M... Alaïa?"

He purposely said my name last to make it seem like I wasn't the reason for him being here. His ass wasn't slick. He might've had his new bitch fooled, but I knew him better than he knew himself.

Speaking of his new bitch, Tika was staring daggers at me like she wanted to throw hands. "I'm good. But I think something may be wrong with your bitch. Seems to me she has an eye problem."

"Bitch, you 'bout to have an ass problem when I kick that mothafucka—" Zane quickly grabbed his girl before she swung on me.

"A chicken always clucks! Take yo ghetto ass on somewhere! The way you're acting is unbecoming," I teased, throwing in the new phrase I'd learned from a certain someone.

With cameras surrounding us, the last thing I wanted was to get into a street brawl, but I did, however, get a kick out of fucking with the chick. She hated me because of my status, success and the fact that Zane was still very much so in love with me. Every other week, she was in his phone, finding texts he sent me, basically begging for a taste of this sweet pussy. And every time, she'd blow me up, cursing me out and telling me to stay away as though I were the one begging him. I swear, their silly asses belonged together.

"*Ghetto*? See, I'm sick of you bitches trying to act all bougie all the mothafucking time!!"

Cameras flashed as she thrashed in Zane's embrace, struggling to get a hold of my long Brazilian hair.

"Look at you. Acting a hot, hood ass mess in this nice, peaceful establishment. This isn't Crenshaw, sweetie."

"ALAÏA!" Zane barked my name in anger. "Stop fanning the fucking flames!"

"Stop popping up where ever I am! You ain't gon' achieve shit by following me around! Plus, you need to keep that bitch of yours on a leash!"

Out of nowhere, Tika broke free and charged at me full-speed, fists swinging. She was just about to punch me when someone suddenly grabbed her arm in mid-strike. "Violence of any kind will not be tolerated in this establishment," the owner told her. "In other words, take that shit elsewhere." Flinging her arm like a piece of unwanted trash, he pointed towards the exit, signaling for them to leave.

"Zane, what the hell? You gon' let this fuck nigga grab all on me?" Tika yelled, ready to pounce on him.

Zane looked like wanted to say something in her defense, but decided against it—which was strange for someone as tenacious as him. "Man, fuck this bullshit ass spot. He better hope I don't come back and blow this bitch up." Snatching Tika up, he stalked out in a haze of betrayed confusion

Once they were gone, I turned to my savior to thank him. If it weren't for his interference, I would've surely gotten my ass handed to me. I might have talked a big game but I was a suburban bitch who couldn't fight worth a lick. "Thank you. I really appreciate it. I—"

"I don't know what the fuck you thanking me for. You can see your way outta here too, ma," he spat. "You're a troublemaker and a bad look for business. So get the fuck out my face 'cuz you don't stand a chance getting in this mothafucka again."

2

ALAÏA

Me and my girls parted ways after being kicked out of the nightclub. It was the first time something that embarrassing had ever happened to me, and they were salty that I'd killed the lively vibe. If I hadn't come at Tika sideways, we'd all still be having fun right now. But I just couldn't let that bitch have her way with me.

Ugh!

"Who the fuck did that nigga think he was kicking me out of his club? He obviously doesn't own a TV, or else he'd know who the hell I am! The nerve of his ass! I swear to God, if I run into him again, I will spit in his fucking face!" I laughed under my breath. "Now that'll be a story for the media to gossip about. I can see the headlines now. 'Actress chucks glob of mucus in the face of pompous club owner.' *Hmph*. It would definitely serve him right. Stupid, cocky bitch. I swear these men will be the death of me!"

Massaging my temple, I pulled out my phone and scanned the news to see if anyone was already blogging about me and Tika's altercation. To my puzzled surprise, people were more focused on the fact that I was taking selfies with a bug on my shirt. Apparently, the little fan I posed with had uploaded the pic to her Instagram. It immediately went viral, and sparked a drag session of people ripping me to shreds. Eyes brimming with tears, I read a few of the scathing comments.

No one told me Alaïa starred in A Bug's Life.

How yo money clean but yo clothes dirty? Take a fucking bath, you contaminated culture vulture.

Alaïa's the new lead singer of the Beetles.

Pussy so rotten it be attracting bugs, beetles, and fleas.

My heart broke more and more with each and every scathing comment that I read. I was in the backseat of my chauffeured Escalade on my way home, but suddenly, I didn't feel like being there alone. I knew that if I was, I would only continue to stool in sadness, self-pity and misery.

Closing out the app, I dialed Miracle's number to vent but was sent straight to voicemail. Next, I hit up Chloè, but she too, ignored my phone call. Those bitches were obviously still in their feelings about me getting them kicked out of the club. It wasn't my fault that guy was a total asshole!

Ugh! Damn him!

Because of his stupid ass, I would have to face the tornado of criticism alone. People couldn't begin to understand how stressful stardom could be. I was always under the media's microscope, being judged and picked apart by people that didn't even know me.

One minute fans loved me and the next they were talking shit about me. Being famous was nice and all, but it also came with its fair share of baggage. Baggage that would drive the average person insane. People always assumed that being a celebrity was all about the glitz and glam, but what they failed to see off camera was the bullshit and scrutiny that came along with it.

"Oh well. Fuck 'em. One week, they love you. Next week, they hate you. Both weeks, I got paid."

***

Thirty minutes later, my driver pulled up to the entrance of the building I lived in. I'd recently moved into a beautiful, corner unit penthouse after receiving some hate mail back at my old residence. Like Miracle had pointed out, there were some crazed ass fans who would do just about anything to get my attention— including scaring the ever-loving shit out of me. The letter from the creep said that he'd break into my home when I was asleep, kidnap me, beat me, and then impregnate me. It was some sick twisted shit, but to avoid such a thing happening, I beefed up my security and moved to a more private location. With concierge, gated access, and 24-

hour police officers on sight, the chances of someone getting in this bitch to cause bodily harm to me were slim next to none.

After letting myself in, I greeted concierge and made my way up to the 30th floor. As soon as the elevator opened on my level, I automatically froze in place. Standing a mere few inches from my apartment door was the last person I expected to see.

What the fuck is he doing here, I wondered.

"I should've known that bullshit display at your club was just a front to get me to leave! Did your pervy ass follow me here?!" I yelled. "To get me alone—You fucking creep, is that what you do to chicks you hit on? Huh? Kick them out of your club and follow them home? How fucking pathetic can you be?!"

The owner of the nightclub shook his head in irritation.

"Don't ignore me, you piece of shit! Answer me before I call the cops!"

"Call them," he insisted. "I have every right to be here, just as you."

"The hell you do! I'm the one who lives h—
"

Before I could finish my rant, he slammed the door in my face, once again leaving me speechless and dumbfounded. Up until now, I had no idea that he was my next-door neighbor. I'd only been living here a few weeks, so this was my first time ever seeing another resident on my floor.

What were the odds that my neighbor would be him? It almost seemed like someone was playing a bad joke on me. Surely, this had to be some sort of prank.

First, he kicks me out of his club, then I find out he lives next to me?

How the fuck was that even possible? And why did he leave the club right after me? Was it so that I could discover he was my neighbor...to make my night even worse?

Dismissing him and the coincidence from my thoughts, I stormed into my apartment and slammed the door shut behind me. Alone in the dark, I turned my music on, poured a glass of Sangria and drowned myself in my sorrows.

Shortly after, I found myself scrolling through the comments of every gossip blog dragging me for the selfie with the roach on my shirt. I didn't know why I continued to torture myself by reading them, but for some reason, I just couldn't seem to stay away.

When is this bitch's 15 minutes of fame gonna be over?

Bury her ass with the Kardashians!

Why couldn't that beetle have been poisonous to spare us from her bad ass acting?

You know yo fans don't fuck with you when they refuse to tell you that you have a cockroach on your shirt.

That dirty bitch needs to crawl back up in the pussy that should've aborted her.

I hate Alaïa! That's what her stupid, overrated, no-talent having ass gets!

Tossing my phone, I buried my face in the couch and sobbed hysterically. "WHAT THE FUCK!"

3

L

Polishing the barrel of my sniper rifle, I listened to my annoying ass neighbor sob hysterically while drunkenly singing along to Xscape's "*Who Can I Run To*"? Her music was loud as hell and she was terribly off-key. It also didn't help that the walls were paper thin, or perhaps it was my acute, preternatural hearing abilities that made her sound like she was right next to me. Either way, the bitch was getting on my last nerves.

It took everything in me not to go over there and shove that speaker down her fucking throat. Shit was getting out of hand. I was 'bout to pull up on a nigga and I needed every bit of concentration to focus on this task. It was why I'd left the club in the first place. I had to swap professions for a brief moment. No one knew it, but outside of being an entrepreneur and businessman, I made my real living as a professional hitman. The nightclubs I owned were just a front for tax purposes.

The white couple I was politicking with earlier were long-term clients of mine. Any problems they had, I'd see about, for the right price of course, and they were always generous in their contributions. A single job alone could run you half a mil, but they graciously doubled the amount whenever I handled their "situations".

Recently, their teenage son was involved in a fellow student's suicide. He and a couple of his friends had been bullying the victim until he finally gave in and decided to take the easy way out. Instead of letting their son rot in prison, they paid to have me execute the only witness in his upcoming trial.

I wasn't biased when it came to taking assignments so I humbly accepted. When you killed for a living, you had no space in your heart for emotions or empathy. I'd pop a baby or an old lady if the price was right. When it came to this paper, I didn't discriminate.

After wiping down my F2 Sniper Rifle, I grabbed the envelope my clients had passed to me at the club and read over the details. Everything I needed to know was all typed up and perfectly outlined for me. Eighteen-year-old, Jason Harper was my target.

His parents were out of town for the weekend and he was throwing a house party while they were away. The distraction was just what I needed to make my move.

Five-hundred thousand was already deposited into my foreign bank account, and once the gig was finished, I'd have the other half a million waiting on me. This shit was light work to a nigga like me. I'd been doing it so long that killing came naturally. All I knew was kill, kill, kill...

In the beginning, I used to throw up and have nightmares after every job. Now I took lives without even batting an eyelash. I killed with no regard whatsoever to human life. I was a soulless, empty shell of a man that valued no one and nothing more than the millions rolling into my bank account.

"Who can I run tooooo? To share this empty space? Who can I run toooo? When I looooooove?"

My neighbor carried on with her terrible singing and I was actually tempted to shoot her ass instead.

"I know love has many meanings and a message very clear! All it takes is time and patience...to bring you nearrrrr! But who got me?!"

Sighing in frustration, I looked at the wall that was most likely connected to her living room.

"Who can I run to? I need looooooove!"

My expression softened as she suddenly broke down crying again. The bitch was a real pain in my ass but for some reason, I felt sorry for the girl. She had everything most people dreamed of possessing, and yet she was unhappy. She didn't know it, but I'd done my research on her—

prior to our awkward meeting—along with all of the other residents in the building. I was paranoid like that, so I took extra precaution when it came to my surroundings.

Unfortunately, when doing my research, I found nothing about Alaïa that made her likeable. Beautiful and talented, maybe. But likeable...definitely not. She was just as arrogant and profane as she presented herself tonight, and it was very easy to see why people hated her ass.

"*Who can I run to? To fill this empty space?*" she sang.

"No damn body, you keep that act up," I mumbled.

"WHY DO THEY HATE ME?!" she screamed. "Why do they fucking hate me?! One minute, they like me! The next they're talking shit about me! No one's perfect! Why the hell do they expect me to be so fucking perfect?! Why can't they just love me and accept me?! What do I have to do?!" she cried.

Her rants were so loud and dramatic, that I could hear her crystal clear through the paper-thin walls.

"WHAT DO I HAVE TO DO?!"

I chuckled and shook my head. "You could stop being a bitch."

***

Sliding on a full faced armored mask, I studied Jason's home from a secluded vantage point nearby. This would be a quick lick. I wasn't 'bout to be all day with this shit. The sooner I got it done, the better.

Positioning myself so that I was level with his home, I peered through my sniper rifle to get a clear shot of him. Unfortunately, the task was damn near impossible with all of the people surrounding him. Every time, I went to pull the trigger, someone would walk past, fucking up my aim.

Shit!

I had half a mind to lock their asses inside and set that bitch ablaze. Fuck it. If I had to sacrifice a couple dozen casualties to get at Jason, then so be it. These kids meant nothing to me. Whether they lived or died was of no real concern to me.

Resting my finger on the trigger, I followed his every movement through my scope. Before I could take the shot, two friends jumped in front of him and started horsing around in a drunken stupor.

Fucking kids.

I hated kids.

Sighing in frustration, I abandoned the vantage point and slowly made my way towards the house. I'd exhausted Plan A, so I had no choice but to resort to Plan B.

I'mma have to fuck around, break in that bitch, and make that mothafucka RIP.

I didn't mind the second option, because I could stage the death more appropriately, clearing my clients of any and all suspicion. A bullet was just a quick and convenient way of handling shit.

Approaching the estate filled to the brim with teens, I snaked to the side of the house and crept in through the bathroom window—barging right in on a nigga that was taking a piss.

"WHAT THE FUCK—"

I quickly grabbed and slammed his head into the corner of the wall, intending to knock him out but more than likely killing him. I didn't bother to check his pulse as I crept into the hallway, ducking out of view whenever someone walked past. There were people drinking, smoking, dancing and fucking everywhere.

All of a sudden, Jason appeared with some bitch on his arm. He had a blunt in his mouth and a pack of condoms in one hand, like shit was 'bout to go down

Out of respect, I gave him 10 minutes to handle his business before I put this hammer on his ass, but he didn't even need five. When the chick finally walked out of the room unsatisfied and angry, I caught her off guard, tossed her back into the bedroom and kicked the door shut behind me.

She jumped up and tried to run and a brief scuffle ensued, which ended with her knocking off my mask. Tossing her ass into the dresser, she smacked her head and fell to the floor, unconscious. Finally realizing the severity of the situation, Jason jumped up and reached for the nightstand, where I presumed a weapon was inside. Now that he'd seen my mothafucking face, it ain't no way I could let that bitch continue to walk around.

POP!

I blew his fingers off with the nine I was carrying, stopping his ass in his tracks. He barely had a second to register the pain before I put two in his head and one in his chest. The nigga looked ridiculous with his dick out, so I did him a favor by pulling the sheets over his body.

Walking back over to the unconscious girl, I moved her body to the middle of the room and placed the gun in her hand. You would've thought I was a director, prepping a scene for filming; I wanted this shit to look so legit. Now when police discovered Jason's body, they'd think he was killed in retaliation for raping her. It was the perfect setup.

After putting my mask back on, I left the bedroom, slipped through the bathroom window and disappeared into the darkness. Like I said, this shit was light work to a nigga like me. I'd been doing it so long and so proficiently that killing was second nature to me.

***

The following afternoon, I bumped into Alaïa in the hallway on my way out. She was standing at the entrance of her apartment in a much better mood than last night, admiring the gifts in front of her door. The smile on her face was from ear-to-ear as she fawned over the roses, stuffed animals, and cards.

"What the fuck is all this shit in the hallway?" I spat. "You know this is a fire hazard. Clean this shit up before I report you to management."

"I'm just now seeing it. Stop being so grouchy! I'm bringing it inside. Damn."

I scoffed in irritation. "Well, hurry the hell up. It's a fucking eye sore."

"Fuck you!"

"I can imagine you're quite the hoarder getting shit like that every day."

"Why do you care what's in my place? Huh? You ain't paying my mothafucking mortgage!"

"Well, I wish you'd pay it elsewhere. You were a pain in my ass in the club and you a pain in my ass as a neighbor. So do me a favor and just stay the hell away from me, aight...And keep that bullshit out of my walkway. I don't wanna be tripping over that shit every other fucking day."

Alaïa tossed her hair over her shoulder. The bitch was so Hollywood. "You are such a fucking hater. Don't be mad that people love me and appreciate me. If you were as beautiful and as talented as me, then so would you. Maybe if you were a bit nicer, you'd have some fans of your own. I heard how women avoid you like the plague." She smirked. "Now I see why. You're a total fucking asshole. What type of bitch would want that?"

Her weak ass attempt at prying into my personal life was not going to work. Without giving her the satisfaction of responding, I walked right past her towards the elevators.

"Oh, so now you don't have shit to say?" she challenged.

"I said all I had to say," I tossed over my shoulder. "Keep that shit out of my walkway or I'm reporting your ass."

Before she could respond, the elevator doors closed, giving me the separation that I desperately needed. Being around her made me nervous, anxious, and unbalanced—the total opposite of how I normally was. Chuckling to myself, I shook my head in disbelief. Alaïa was really something else...

This bitch was a mothafucking pain my ass...but why did my heart start racing whenever she was around? Why was I so taken with her smile? And why did I get those damn flowers, cards, and gifts for her, pretending to be her fans? I was breaking every damn rule in the book for this girl, without really knowing why.

4

CHLOÈ

Standing in the doorway of the master bathroom, I stared at the trick I was never supposed to fall in love with. Bruce Hanley was a 62-year old wealthy real estate tycoon that used to fuck with my mother in the 70s—back when she was beautiful and lively—as he'd often say. But when she got too old and used up to hold his interest, she passed him off to me.

My mother knew how much he loved young, tight pussy, so she seized the opportunity to pimp out her only child. The money and luxuries Bruce showered me with was enough to keep us both happy, and he provided us with a life that we could never afford on our own.

The mansion in Beverly Hills we lived in was in his name. The myriad of foreign cars we pushed were leased by him. The designer clothes we flaunted were on his dime. Bruce had me and my mother living like Kris and Kim Kardashian, and he made sure that we never wanted for anything.

Don't get too invested in your emotions, my mom would always say. *He's just a trick, remember that. And a trick is only good for one thing, and it ain't falling in love.*

Regardless of her materialistic ideology, I allowed myself to do just that. Not only was Bruce the love of my life, he was also like a father figure to me. I was never close to my own, so to me, he was the closest thing to it because he took care of me and instilled in me a wisdom that was far beyond my years.

You see, Bruce was an OG. Back in the 60s and early 70s, he was the biggest kingpin the west coast had ever seen. Moving coca from Cuba by the keys, he supplied all of California as well as Southwestern America. The nigga was a legend and once served 20 years in the Fed, for a couple murder charges he'd caught during his reign. But that was back in the day. Back when he was running the drug game; back when my mama was his side bitch.

Now Bruce was retired, investing his money into companies instead of cocaine. He owned businesses, properties, stocks, and a few non-profit organizations that boosted his squeaky-clean image. In other words, he was a square—but he was a paid ass square, so I didn't mind. Besides, he treated me like royalty. Like a queen...and better than his own wife.

Sauntering towards the bed, I gazed at him longingly and lovingly. Like I was the bitch he'd put a ring on some thirty years ago instead of Irene Hanley. It didn't matter though. Even if we weren't bounded by vows, we were still banded by loyalty. Bruce was my nigga; my soulmate—

regardless of me not having the slip of paper to prove it. I was his bitch till the day that I expired...or at least until he got tired and replaced me the same way he did Mama. However, I knew that if I fucked and sucked him good enough, I wouldn't have anything to worry about anytime soon.

"Why you lookin' at me like that, Pretty Mama," he smiled, just as handsome as he was forty or so years ago. To be in his early sixties, the man was remarkably attractive with salt and pepper hair, a lean frame, hazel eyes, and chiseled jawline. The fact that he could still get it up was just an added bonus.

Tiptoeing to the bed, I climbed on top and mounted him. He'd been calling me Pretty Mama ever since I was given to him at the ripe age of 16. He was the one who took my virginity. And while there were other tricks out there who paid for my time and attention, none of them possessed my heart like Bruce. He was more than just a sugar daddy. He was my everything.

"Because I love you." I brought his hand up to my lips and kissed it. I didn't give a fuck if he was wearing his wedding band. He never once hid the fact that he was married. He was open, honest, and upfront, and because of that, I had no choice but to respect him as a man. Most niggas couldn't be real about their shit.

"Show me..." he said, rubbing my ass. There wasn't much, but what little I had, he paid for. He even purchased my lips, titties, nose, and eye color change. Anything I wanted Daddy gave me. He'd do whatever to keep a smile on my face.

Sliding down his frame, I stopped at the waistline of his dress pants and unbuckled his Hermes belt. We had a huge suite all to ourselves at the Hotel Roosevelt, thanks to his business relationship with the owner. Our shit had a kitchenette, patio, and in-door Jacuzzi with the mini bar.

His wife was under the impression that he was out of town on business. But what she didn't know was that he was actually caked up with his side bitch in Hollywood. He'd told me all about how her pussy couldn't get wet anymore, so I knew that she wasn't taking care of him the way that he ought to be, but it was impossible when you weren't equipped with the necessary tools. Fortunately, I was able to give Bruce everything that bitch couldn't and more—including some fire ass head. Speaking of which, I was about to bestow upon him some of the best he'd ever experienced.

Easing Bruce's enormous cock through the opening of his boxers, I kissed the tip and smacked it gently against my cheek. Pre-cum smeared across my skin as I slid it between my pert breasts. Smashing them together, I proceeded to titty-fuck the shit out of him, every so often, dripping spit on his dick to lubricate it. I knew how much Bruce loved that shit, and it was evident from the way he moaned and moved about.

"*Mmm.* Chloè...Shit," he groaned, grabbing the back of my head. "Put some more spit on it, baby."

I sucked and drooled on the tip of his dick, coating it in thick saliva before taking it whole in my mouth. Watching my head bob up down, he grabbed the small plastic bag off the nightstand and popped a Viagra. He didn't need the shit, but he liked to take them anyway because he loved to fuck me until the sun rose. He thought since he was three times my age, he had to go all out to please me but that wasn't the case. Still, I never argued with his choice to use it, just like he never argued with my choice to pop painkillers. We reserved our judgment, never putting the other down for their own personal decisions. That's what I loved most about our relationship. We accepted each other for who we were.

"You like that, Daddy?" I moaned. "You like the way I polish that dick?"

Wrapping a hand around my hair, Bruce guided my head up and down his length. "Fuck yeah..."

My tongue glided luxuriously along the sensitive spots of his cock. Bruce moaned uncontrollably, running his fingers through my long hair, eyes shut tightly in overwhelming satisfaction.

His balls tightened as my mouth sped up, my tonsils smashing into the tip of his dick, as I forced all he had to offer down my throat. Bruce might've been an old man, but the nigga was well-equipped.

I was forced to swallow several times as his cock steadily oozed out a thick stream of pre-cum, releasing all of his back-up due to his wife's neglect. Sucking and slobbering on his dick like a porn star, I jacked it a little here and there. No more than two minutes later, his dick twitched and erupted with a boatload of cum. I nearly gagged because it was so fucking much.

When I pulled his dick from my mouth, my face and lips were dripping with nut. Bruce pulled me up on his body and kissed me sloppily in the mouth, cleaning my face of his own cum. The nigga was a certified freak, but I loved that shit.

After getting his first nut, he flipped me over and slid between my legs. He had about five more orgasms in him, compliments of the pill he'd popped. Knowing him, my pussy would probably be sore after tonight, but as long as the pain was accompanied by pleasure, it was well-worth it to me.

Pushing his pole deep inside of me, he rammed into my pussy with the agility of a man half his age. "Oh, shit! Bruce! Fuck me!" I bellowed, pussy creaming uncontrollably. "Damn, baby. Get this pussy, Daddy. Get it!"

Thrusting his hips in a powerful fashion, he pounded into me over and over. "Shit, Pretty Mama." He gasped. "This is some...good pussy..."

All of a sudden, his eyes shot open in surprise—and what looked like joy—and then suddenly, he collapsed on top of me.

Laughing in amusement, I looked down at him and smiled, "Damn, baby, already?" I just knew he had a few more rounds in him.

Bruce was silent.

"Baby...Get up," I giggled. "You have to get me off now. I'm still horny."

No response.

"Bruce, baby...?"

Suddenly, I realized he wasn't moving.

Panic-stricken, I quickly shook him violently to wake him up! "Bruce?! Oh my God, Bruce?! Baby, please get up!" I cried. "Don't do this to me, Daddy! Please don't do this to me!"

Crying and screaming for help, it quickly dawned on me that Bruce had succumbed to a fatal heart-attack.

5

L

"It's done."

There was a long pause on the other end of the line before the elder women finally responded. "Very well. I'll have my accountant wire the remaining balance."

"Excellent. A pleasure doing business with you." After hanging up the phone, I lit a Newport and took a few puffs. The world could be so cruel. Thirty years married to a mothafucka, and the wife pays me to murk the nigga. Between the two of us, I didn't know who was more savage.

Poor Bruce had no idea that the Viagra he'd popped was actually a fake. Unbeknownst to him, I'd switched out the medication with pills that were laced with a traceless and toxic poison. I didn't just kill by using guns. I had all types of tactical ways to eliminate a target. Some more severe than others.

When Irene Hanley reached out to me weeks ago, demanding that she wanted her cheating husband killed for insurance purposes, I had no qualms about doing my part. After all, I didn't discriminate. I had this murder game on lock.

***

When I finally made it back to the apartment building, I bumped into Alaïa once again in the hallway. She was on her way out the door; where ever she was going, I didn't give a fuck.

From the corner of my eye, I caught a glimpse of the short ass mini skirt she had on. Okay, so maybe I did give a fuck...but it was of no real importance to me. She could walk off the roof to her death and I still wouldn't stop her. Getting caught up with a bitch like Alaïa would only cause problems for me, and with my life and occupation, I just simply didn't have time for it.

"Good evening, Mr. Grouchy," she greeted with a cheery smile. All that fan-love must've gotten to her big ass head.

I didn't respond, or acknowledge the fact that her bright effervescence brought light into my cold, dark world.

"Can't speak?" she asked at my ungracious non-welcome.

Ignoring her question, I let myself into my apartment and slammed the door right in her fucking face.

"Well, fuck you too," I heard her say.

Alaïa could hate a nigga all she wanted, but at the end of the day, she was better off without me. My black, empty heart was completely void of warmth and kindness. There was no room for fondness or friendship. I had a strong, mental fortitude about myself. This contract killing shit had hardened me. I was a fucked up cocktail of a human being. So cold and uncaring that I couldn't even fathom the thought of learning to love a woman. When it came to romance, I was pretty much hopeless in that department. When you killed for a living, you had no time for such trivial, superficial bullshit. All that mattered to me was the count and the amount. All of the other shit was just that...

6

MIRACLE

BOOM!

BOOM!

BOOM!

I was giving myself a facial when someone started pounding on my front door like the LAPD. I almost thought it was until I realized they had no real reason to come to the Hollywood Hills. Security was tight around here. People couldn't even drive through this mothafucka without permitted access.

I rented a beautiful home in the Hills, away from the hustle and bustle of Los Angeles. It was quiet, safe, and only a handful of people knew where I laid my head. Needless to say, I was a bit surprised to find Zane standing on my doorstep. I'd never told his ass where I lived after moving from my last place, but it wasn't hard for a nigga like him to pull some strings to track a bitch down. Apparently, whatever he had to say must've been important since he couldn't just text the shit.

"What the hell are you doing here?" I asked.

"Damn. No invite?" he said, barging inside.

"You were coming in whether you had one or not."

"Bitch, you damn right," he shot back. "Who the fuck was that nigga all over Alaïa at the club last night? And if you tell me he a friend, I'mma smack the fuck outta you."

"*All over Alaïa?*" I laughed. "Nigga, you need to leave that Molly alone, 'cuz me and you saw two different things. The man only intervened to keep yo ratchet ass bitch from tearing Alaïa's tracks out. Something that *you* should've been doing! But instead you brought your messy ass there, hoping for some shit to pop off. Now you here asking me if Alaïa's fucking that nigga." I laughed and shook my head in astonishment. "Do you even think before you act, Zane? Do you even consider the consequences or outcome of your actions?"

"Man, miss me with all that shit. It was a simple ass question."

"I don't have the answers, Z. Maybe you should get them from Alaïa."

Sensing my attitude, Zane snatched me up in anger. "Bitch, what the fuck is yo problem? Get out'cho feelings, ho. We ain't fucking no more. Fuck outta here with all that bullshit."

"*Fucking?* Is that all it was to you?! Mothafucka, I loved yo ass!"

Zane turned me loose after hearing those three words. You would've thought they were fire searing his skin. "Bitch, I done told you to stop saying that bullshit."

"Well, how am I supposed to feel?" I cried, tears pouring down my cheeks. "I was in love with you before Alaïa even looked your way! You told me one day it'd be us sitting on top of the world, but all you fed me was lies and bullshit! I stayed down for you, Z! I never told Alaïa about us! Betrayed my own best friend for you—and you played me! Now you running around the city with that Tika bitch when it should be me! ME! I was the one who hit that lick in 2013, so you could invest in this rap shit! Mothafucka, I been A-1 since day one! And yet you treat me like you don't even know me! Like our past never existed! That's fucked up, Z! That's real fucked up!"

"Man, we been over this shit!" he yelled. "I done already told you shit be complicated!"

"Why?" I demanded. "Why is it so complicated? Why can't we just come out to the world together? Say fuck what everyone thinks and just be happy?"

"Bitch, I'mma mothafucking mogul. A nigga can't just do that shit."

"Why?" I cried. "Because of Alaïa...or because you don't want people to know you're a trade?"

Zane shot an evil glare my way. The truth hurt.

"Answer me!" I hollered. "It's because I'm a tranny, right?!"

"Bitch, that ain't got shit to do with it—"

"Stop lying—"

"Yo, you trippin'. I'mm holla at'chu when you out'cho feelings. I ain't got time for this bullshit right now."

Dropping to my knees in the middle of the floor, I broke down crying as I watched him leave. For the last 7 years, he'd been walking in and out of my life. He'd treat me good behind closed doors, but hid me from society out of sheer embarrassment. It wasn't fair for me to continue being his dirty, little secret.

I deserved loved. I deserved a happily ever after with the man that I cherished and adored. Why did he insist on hiding in the closet...and hiding me, as well? It wasn't fair!

"Zane!" I cried out. "Zane, baby, I'm sorry! Come back! ZANE!"

7

CHLOÈ

Covered in tears and dried up nut, I dragged my feet up the stairs leading to the front door of my mansion. Before I could even stick the key in the door, it went flying open on its own. Claire Moreau appeared in a flannel Valentino pants suit and curly wig. Every day my mother wore a different style, and every year, she spent over 2 million dollars having custom wigs designed. Her addiction was just as bad as mine was to painkillers.

Staring daggers at me, she squinted her eyes in disapproval and folded her arms. She and I shared a striking resemblance with our butterscotch skin, sharp feline features, and modelesque figures. My mother was 51 but could easily pass for 30.

"How dare you show up here," she said through ever-so-slightly gritted teeth.

Right away, I was confused. "Mama, I—"

WHAP!

Without warning, she slapped the shit out of me, causing my ankle to twist. I toppled down the flight of stairs and landed on my funny bone. A jolt of pain shot throughout my entire body. I'd never experienced anything more severe in all my life.

"How dare you show up here after what you did to Bruce! After what you did to me!"

"But Mama, Bruce had a heart attack!" I cried. She was acting like I murdered him. I would never intentionally harm Bruce, I loved him. "It wasn't my fault!"

"The hell it wasn't!! It's all over the fucking news!" she shouted. "*Wealthy real estate tycoon found dead with hooker*! HOOKER!" she laughed cynically. "That's what the news reporters are calling you! Do you know how embarrassing that is?! How much of a disgrace you are to me?!" My mother kicked my leg. "Answer me, bitch! Do you?!"

"Mama, I'm sorry—"

She cut me off with her strategic process of picking me apart. "I agree. You are sorry. A sorry ass excuse for a daughter!" she hollered. "If your dumb ass had fucked him into putting a ring on your finger, we'd be sitting on that 200-million-dollar life insurance policy, instead of Irene's fat ass! That and any other assets and inheritances would be ours! But instead we get zero! Nada!" she screamed. "TEN YEARS! Ten years you been sucking the dust out that dick and what do you have to show for it! NOTHING!"

Tears streamed down my cheeks as she shredded my soul with her razor-sharp tongue. It was already bad enough having to deal with Bruce dying on top of me. Now I had to face the wrath of a scorned, greedy, overbearing mother.

"Well, I'll tell you what, bitch, it's back to square one for you!" Before I could argue with her, she grabbed me by the hair and snatched me to my feet. "You better get your bleached ass back out there and find another John to support this family because them tricks you got on standby ain't worth shit but a handbag and a pair of shoes! You better scour the streets of LA, little girl! And don't bring your ass back till you find another Bruce Hanley or someone of equal value!"

"Mama, please!" I sobbed. "I'm tired. I just wanna take a shower and go to bed—"

"You can sleep when you die!" She shoved me in the direction of my car. "Right now you need to find another nigga to put food on this table! This mothafucking mortgage ain't gon' pay itself! We done came too far! I ain't going back to Carson!"

There were tears in her eyes after her last statement. My mother's biggest fear was returning to the hood. She'd sell my soul if that kept her living the Hollywood high life, and that's exactly what she was doing to me. Selling my soul to the highest bidder.

"Go to the Grove!" she demanded. "Go hang out at LA Live or Fleming's or the JW Marriott! I think there's a Lakers game tonight! Yo ass need to be all up and down that strip! And if there's no luck there, go to Catch, Above Sixty, or any of the upscale bars in Hollywood! There's so many places to snag a baller in LA, it ain't even funny!" she said. "If you come back empty-handed, then that only means you ain't try hard enough! And if you don't try hard enough, then yo ass ain't welcome here!" she snarled. "So don't come back this way until you find another steady paycheck!"

After tearing me to shreds, she stomped up the stairs and slammed the door in my face. The least she could've done was let me wash my musty pussy. My mother was so concerned about where her next meal was coming from that she didn't even care about what I was going through mentally. A man that I loved and cared about had just died on me. My life would never be the same. As a mother, I needed her to hug me and tell me that everything was going to be okay, but instead she tossed me to the wolves like a piece of fucking meat. To retain her wealth, she'd sacrifice anything including her own daughter.

"This just ain't no way to live," I cried. "This ain't no mothafucking way to live!"

8

ALAÏA

What the fuck is that nigga's deal, I asked myself for the hundredth time. *Why is he always so cold and cynical with me?*

Chewing on my pen cap, I daydreamed about the unequivocal villain next door to me, and the reason behind his brusque demeanor. His attitude was mostly detached with a sprinkling of bitterness, and he was devoid of any warmth. Why was he always in this grumpy mood?

I was supposed to be looking over a script and jotting down a few notes for my upcoming audition, but for some strange reason, he lingered in my thoughts.

The more he curved me, the more I craved him...or so that's how it seemed. Normally, men found my charm and good looks irresistible and yet, here he was, swatting away my advances like I was some annoying fly. What was it about me that he didn't like? Surely, he wasn't still holding a grudge about that night in his club?

No. He couldn't be, I convinced myself.

A dozen thoughts bounced around in my empty echoing skull.

Standing to my feet, I sauntered over towards the full-length mirror in my bedroom and looked myself over. Even with my reading glasses on, I was impeccably beautiful. Smooth honey-colored skin, high cheekbones, pouty lips, piercing brown eyes, long legs and a curvaceous figure. I was untouchable!

Women adored me and men worshipped me through social media fan pages. I knew because I read the comments whenever I was down to make me feel better about myself. Smiling in admiration, I took in all of my features and everything that made me the dynamic superstar that I was.

"That nigga *must* be gay," I told myself. "No way in *hell* he thinks I'm not a bad bitch."

Turning around, I looked at my ass and frowned in disappointment. It wasn't big but it wasn't small, definitely nothing to write home about. All of a sudden, my insecurities came crashing down like a ton of bricks.

Perhaps I'm too skinny for him. Maybe he likes them thick, Corn-Fed Georgia women with asses big enough to serve a meal on. I shook my head and laughed at the thought. *Oh, well if he does. I don't know why I'm tripping anyway. He ain't even that cute.*

Suddenly, his handsome chiseled face popped into my head. A smile came to mind when

I pictured him scowling at me in the sexy ass way that he did whenever he complained. Who the hell was I kidding? That nigga was fine as fuck!

Caramel skin, bedroom eyes, rough but delicate facial features, and that body! Good God, that body! Every time, I saw the brother, his muscles were bulging through his three-piece suits. He was classy, sophisticated, mysterious, and charming in a pushy kind of way. But regardless of the manner he talked to me in, I couldn't deny that there was something fascinating about him. Something that drew me to him. Something that was unexplainable. His actions had a chastening effect, despite how unpleasant he was.

"Dammit, Alaïa, focus!" I scolded myself. "Get your head in the fucking game!"

Miracle had gone to bat for me to get this role and I couldn't let her down by blowing it. I had to put those thoughts of him behind me for now and pay attention to the task at hand. Opportunities like these came once in a lifetime.

***

After a brief pep-talk, I left the apartment to get some coffee downstairs in the cyber café. I wasn't particularly fond of it, but I needed a quick pick-me-up to focus on the script I was studying.

On the way to the coffee machine, I caught a glimpse of the brother hitting weights in the gym. It was connected to the cyber café, so it wasn't hard to miss. I got all fluttery with excitement when I noticed it was my next door neighbor. The moment I saw him, my chest tingled. He was shirtless and wearing a pair of gray sweatpants—

After zeroing in on his crotch region, my jaw hit the floor. Homeboy was holding heat! It looked like he was hiding a snake in that mothafucka, his dick was so gotdamn big.

Oh, my Lord. My sweet, heavenly Father.

He had me thinking lusty thoughts.

Muscles and six-pack bulging, he lifted the dumbbells, causing every vein in his body to push up against his skin. He was a hulking mass of man, ripped to perfect, glowing with sweat and unwavering determination. *Damn.* He was so fucking fine. One look at him and you could tell that he was a disimpassioned heartbreaker.

My eyes slowly wandered down to the bottom of his sweats, where the ends were rolled up, exposing his awesome calve muscles. He was slightly bowlegged, a secret weakness of mine.

He looks even taller when he's half naked, I thought. The man had to be at least 6"3 or maybe even 6"4. He was lean and powerfully built like a basketball player. *I wonder if he used to play*, I found myself inquiring.

Shit!

As soon as he turned in my direction, I quickly ducked out of sight. I didn't want him seeing me in my pajama pants, baggy shirt, and glasses. I looked a hot, homely mess! Funny how just a few minutes ago, I was praising my good looks. Now, I didn't think so highly of myself. Just being in his presence humbled me.

After making sure the coast was clear, I rushed back up to my floor, changed into a tight ass pair of yoga pants and slipped into a sports bra. Ten minutes later, I entered the gym with intentions of finally being noticed by him. Instead of coming off desperate or thirsty, I tried to play it low-key.

He was doing curls on the work-out bench, so I decided to hit the treadmill while pretending I didn't see him. I figured if I didn't chase him, he'd come running to me. At least, that's what my mama would always say.

Is he looking?

From the corner of my eye, I stole a glance at the mirror and caught him watching my ass. A playful grinned tugged at my lips, because I knew a nigga was gon' be a nigga. He couldn't resist how luscious my booty looked in the pair of gray and yellow yoga pants.

When our eyes locked briefly, he quickly cleared his throat and stood to his feet. "Your posture's all wrong. I can tell you really don't do cardio."

"Well, how's it supposed to be, Mr. Fitness Trainer?" My tone was snarky and sarcastic. We had a bickering dynamic similar to Tom and Jerry's.

"Well...for starters...I noticed that you hopped right on and started doing a light jog. You didn't stretch beforehand, and you didn't warm up your joints first with a five to ten-minute walk. Your joints and muscles work best when they're warmed up," he said. "Get that blood flowing by walking at a slow pace on a slight incline. That'll help you avoid muscle strains and tears."

"Oh, so you *can* be kind and helpful," I smiled.

"Don't misread this random act of kindness," he said. "The way I feel about you hasn't changed."

I laughed at his petty behavior. "And how do you feel about me?"

"I feel like you're troublesome."

"And I feel like you're a fucking asshole...but we're neighbors. So, we should at least try to be nice to each other."

He scoffed in disagreement. "*Nice?*" he repeated.

My heart rate increased as he slowly approached me—and it had nothing to do with my speed on the treadmill.

"You don't take me as someone who likes to play nice," he said.

"I can be nice," I argued, almost believing the lie as it fell from my lips. "I mean, we're neighbors. We should at least be respectful of one another."

All of a sudden, he pressed the pause button on the treadmill, nearly causing me to fly into the interface.

There was a brief flicker of surprise in his expression. "Why?" he asked.

Feeling the tension between us, I climbed off the treadmill and backed up a little. He made me nervous and antsy with his close proximity. It was as if I were afraid my body would act on its own volition. Seeing him shirtless and glistening in sweat had me feeling some type of way— especially since it'd been 2 years since the last time I had some.

My clit tingled behind the thin fabric of my panties, reminding me that I'd been depriving her for far too long. *Damn, why did he have to look so good? And why was he staring at me with those bedroom eyes of his like he wanted to devour me?* Everything about him captivated me, primarily that bulge in the center of his sweatpants. *This nigga has a fucking horse dick*!

"Why?" he repeated, walking up to me intimidatingly.

From this brief reverie, I came back down to earth. My eyes quickly snapped from his dick up to his intense gaze. I backed up some more, until I bumped into the mirror behind me. There was nowhere to run as he trapped me between his arms. Staring down at me possessively, he waited on a legitimate response.

"Why should I give a fuck about you?"

I was taken aback at the extent of his coldness. With a shaky breath, my gaze darted between his eyes and lips. The close proximity coupled with the scent of his masculinity had me creaming in my panties. I didn't even know the nigga's name, and I wanted to fuck the shit out of him.

I shrieked mentally without letting my face show my uncertainty and panic.

"Is it 'cuz you think I'm feelin' you, in a different kind of way?" he asked.

I went to respond, but my heart lodged in my throat. He had me nervous, anxious, excited, and uncontrollably wet. *Damn*. What the fuck was this man doing to me?

Ever so slowly, he leaned forward, moving in as if he were going to kiss me.

As crazy as it was, I actually wanted him to...and before I knew it, I was closing my eyes, anticipating the moment his tongue slipped into my mouth.

"I hate to break it to you," he said instead. "But you ain't 'een my type of bitch." And with that, he walked out of the gym, leaving me with a wet pussy and wounded pride.

9

CHLOÈ

Staring off into space inside the booth of a hookah lounge, I thought about how my life hadn't been the same ever since Bruce's tragic death. Between his family members constantly playing on my phone, and my mother's incessant bitching, I felt like I was going to go burst at the seams. Everyone was driving me fucking crazy, which was why I decided to take a reprieve from it all by calling up my friends for some much-needed girl time.

Shortly after my arrival, Miracle came bustling through the door in all her magnificent glory. She was dressed fly as fuck in a teal long sleeve turtleneck and mink fur vest. A tan suede skirt hugged her shapely hips, and on her feet, was a pair of light blue Giuseppe heels with the feathered emblem.

"Bitch, you better slay!" I teased, as she walked up and hugged me.

Miracle laughed. "Oh, stop it, sis." Pulling off her Dior sunglasses, she took a seat across from me and swept her curls over her shoulder. "Where's Alaïa?" she asked.

"You know that bougie bitch has to make a grand entrance."

As if on cue, Alaïa sauntered in the lounge with two bodyguards on either side of her. She was doing the most in a floor length rabbit fur coat, pink Gucci pleated dress, and nude Valentino heels. On her head was a pink wool beret. For a simple night out on the town, she was dressed quite ostentatiously. Then again, she wouldn't be Alaïa if she wasn't doing the most.

"Who the fuck does this bitch think she is? Jackie Kennedy?" I laughed.

"Jackie wishes she was as iconic as me," Alaïa bragged, taking her seat. Her bodyguards made themselves scarce, but were still in plain sight, just in case anything popped off. "And I'm still mad at you hoes for switching up on me. Crying and shit over that nightclub, like there ain't a hundred more in LA."

Now that my girls were here, I was anxious to tell them about Bruce's death...but Alaïa just had to make it about her.

"I mean, it wasn't my fault that guy was an asshole. How was I supposed to know he'd kick us the fuck out? It had nothing to do with me and everything to do with his bitch ass ego. If ya'll were gon' be pissed at anybody, it should be his bitch ass—not me! Besides...I needed you hoes that night and you were nowhere to be found."

"Well, right now I need you to shut the fuck up and listen to me!" I blurted out. "Ya'll bitches ain't gon' believe this shit, but Bruce—"

"Fuck your problems and Bruce! Bitch, look at my face!" Alaïa said, snatching off her sunglasses. Dark circles were under her hazel eyes, and she looked like she hadn't slept in days. "I've been up for the past 2 days, bitch, wracking my mind over my next-door neighbor."

Me and Miracle exchanged confused glances. "Your next-door neighbor? The fuck?"

"The mothafucka that kicked us out of his club! You know—you remember! Can you believe that bastard lives next door to me?!"

Miracle chuckled. "I thought it was odd that you randomly brought him up."

"Bitch, why you wracking your brain over him though?" I asked.

"Because, bitch!" she pouted. "I'm trying to fuck with this nigga. I wanna know why he don't fuck with me...I mean what's not to love about me? You know I'm a bad bitch. And you know I got that bag...without the baggage. You know no kids, no relationship...No baby daddy drama. All my priorities are together. I'm practically perfect! And yet, whenever he sees me, it's like he looks right past a bitch. It's like I don't even exist in his world!" Alaïa looked over at Miracle. "He must be gay, right? Please tell me he must be gay! You know these things, don't you?!"

"So, just because I'm a trans, I'm supposed to know whether or not the nigga is on the DL? Bitch, get a life."

"I read somewhere you guys have a gaydar."

Miracle smiled, despite the irritation in her eyes. "First off, love. Don't call us guys."

"So what do you call that between your legs?" Alaïa retorted.

"A bank." Miracle patted her crotch. "A mothafucking bank, bitch. This shit make money, bitch. Nonstop, round the clock. And bitch this pussy get way more dick than yours. And besides, how the fuck am I supposed to know that nigga's sexual orientation? Maybe that's something *you* should ask him. Hell, *you're* the one he's got up all night, bitch...not me."

Her eyes slightly flared with anger. "Bitch, he does not have me up all night!" Alaïa yelled in embarrassment.

"You just told us he's the reason you got those Beetlejuice bags under ya eyes! Girl, stop fronting! You want that nigga to rearrange your guts, ho. It's written all over ya face!" I teased.

Alaïa blushed even more. "I do *not* want him to rearrange my guts," she lied. "Though, I'm certain he's perfectly capable of it."

Miracle gasped. "And how the fuck would you know that?"

"Bitch, I was walking by the gym yesterday and saw him working out in nothing but sweats. On life, bitch, his meat was damn near touching his knee."

"Hung like a fucking horse," Miracle said. "Bitch, you know you couldn't handle that snake all up in them guts."

"Get off that nigga's cock already. You two can ride his dick later'. Right now, I wanna talk about my problem."

"And what is your problem, Chloè?" Alaïa asked uninterestedly.

"Bitch, what you know 'bout Bruce died on top of me last night...in my pussy...balls deep. You think you got problems? Ho, that shit just changed my mothafucking life! On me—the nigga had a heart attack and died right on top of my ass, bitch!"

"Oh my fucking goodness, Chloè...Damn, that shit's crazy," Miracle reached across the table and covered my hand with her own. She saw me on the verge of breaking down and wanted to comfort me. "Damn. Are you serious?"

"As a heart attack...no pun intended."

Taking a break from her usual self-gloating, Alaïa reached in her purse, pulled out a Kleenex, and handed it to me. "Jesus, Chloè. I'm really sorry to hear that. I know how close you two were."

"Bitch, close ain't even the word," I said, dabbing at my tears. "Bruce was like family to me. He took care of me...he was there for me, throughout all of life's major milestones. He paid for my prom, bought my first dream car, put me through film school—even though I ended up dropping out. He was like my father, lover, and best friend all wrapped in one." Unable to hold it in any longer, I broke down crying hysterically.

Miracle and Alaïa rushed to my side to console me.

"And that ain't even the worst part," I continued. "My mother told me not to bring my ass back home till I find another Bruce Hanley. Never mind the fact that my nigga just died on me. All she cares about is where her next meal's coming from."

"So where have you been staying?" Miracle asked.

"In a hotel. I need the time to clear my head—"

"Nonsense, bitch. You're coming to stay with me until you sort this mess out."

"No," I whined. "You know I hate people doing shit for me."

"I'm not people, bitch. I'm your best fucking friend. You're coming to stay with me, end of story," Miracle said with finality.

I was just about to thank her when Tika and her girls came walking into the hookah lounge. Z wasn't with her for once, but the bitch still had trouble written all over her. As soon as she spotted Alaïa, she ambled over with her thot minions like she had a bone to pick.

Oh, shit. Here we go.

"Well, well, well. What are the odds of bumping into your bitch ass again?" Tika said with folded arms.

"Considering the fact that you're following me, pretty slim," Alaïa retorted. "I saw you bitches crammed in that tiny ass Porsche, trying to keep up with me. You hoes been tailing me since I left my apartment. But what I wanna know is...don't you have better shit to do?"

"Yeah, bitch...I do..."

WHAP!

All of a sudden, and without warning, she stole Alaïa right in the face. Before her girls could jump in, I lunged at one of them and Miracle got at the other. A peaceful night out had quickly turned into a full-on street brawl.

Because Alaïa couldn't fight worth a lick, Tika was giving it to her ass while bystanders recorded the entire thing. This shit would be all over TMZ and World Star Hip Hop before morning. I wanted to help my girl but I was too preoccupied with dragging Tika's friend.

Before Tika could cause any serious injuries, Alaïa's security rushed over and broke up the altercation. Her lip and nose were bleeding by the time they finally pulled Tika off, and instead of being angry at her, she lashed out on them.

"Where the fuck was ya'll?!" Alaïa yelled. "LOOK AT MY MOTHAFUCKING FACE! I have an audition in a couple days! How could you let this shit happen to me?! What the fuck do I pay ya'll faggots for?!"

"My sincerest apologies, Ms. Westbrook. We were in the back of the lounge and didn't hear all of the commotion until now—"

"Excuses are like assholes! Everybody has one, and they're all full of shit!" she screamed. "Just get me the fuck out of here!"

"Yeah, bitch! Run off like the lil' ho you are!" Tika taunted. "I told you the next time I saw yo ass, it was on sight, bitch! Let that ass whooping be a reminder to stay the fuck away from Zane!"

"Fuck you and Zane!" Alaïa hollered over her shoulder.

Tika tried to run up again but security stopped her as they quickly whisked Alaïa out of the establishment. One of them tossed his wool coat over her head so that cameras wouldn't catch a glimpse of her bloodied and battered face.

This was supposed to be a drama-free night...but once again Alaïa managed to make it all about her.

10

ALAÏA

On the way up to my apartment, I received a text from Miracle warning me to stay away from social media. That could only mean one thing. That the press had already caught wind of the fight between me and Tika, and they were broadcasting it all over the news outlets.

The drama and negativity in my life were like stains on my career and reputation. Who the hell would want to work with someone that was known for being hot-tempered, violent, and unprofessional? Not only that, but the whole world now knew about me getting my ass kicked. To say that I was embarrassed would've been an understatement. I wanted to die from pure mortification. I was utterly humiliated.

Opening my Instagram app, I went straight to *TheShadeRoom*, where people were dragging me in the comments under the video of our fight. Tears filled my eyes as I skimmed over a few scathing remarks.

Her ass needed a good back-to-Earth beat down.

Dragged her like a carry-on.

That bitch got boxed the fuck down.

She mopped that bitch.

Ole girl rocked her shit. That ho Alaïa straight got muffed.

That bitch knocked out her curls.

Damn. Did you at least pinch the bitch?

That chick caught a bad one lol.

That bitch put the paws on Alaïa. Straight gave that bitch a reality check.

She should've murked that ho. Spare us from her crappy ass movies and TV dramas.

Exiting the app, I shoved my phone in my bag and groaned in frustration. "*UGH!* Gotdamn!" I said, exasperated. I felt like curling up into a tiny, little ball and dying. It was as if the whole world were laughing at me with Tika front and center.

The bitch had no real reason to put her hands on me. It wasn't like I wanted her nigga. Me and Zane were history. The bitch just wanted an excuse to take her insecurities out on me.

Speaking of Zane, I wasn't too surprised when he called me just before I stepped onto the elevator. "What the fuck do you want?" I yelled into the receiver.

"Answers...Why the fuck was you fighting Tika?" he asked.

"Um. Correction. Your bitch was fighting me! I thought I told you to keep that beast on a leash. The bitch has been following me around, waiting for the right moment to pounce! Did you know that? Or were you two busy sniffing behind me?"

"Man, chill with all that. Where you at right now?" he asked, somewhat urgently.

"Where the fuck do you think? At home, where there's no camera crew or ratchet bitches waiting to jump on me!"

"Stay yo ass right there. I'm on my way."

"Nah! Don't come here. What you need to do is see about your bitch, 'cuz I'm 'bout to put the prosecutor on that ass!"

"Man, I done told yo ass to chill. Look, I'm finna pull up. Don't go nowhere. Stay the fuck right there."

Before I could dispute his decision, Zane hung up the phone.

I swear, between him and Tika, I don't know who the hell is driving me crazier.

When I finally made it to my floor, I noticed my neighbor leaving out of his apartment in his usual irascible mood. He was exquisitely dressed to the nines in a navy three-piece and brown alligator skin loafers. He was truly a gifted wearer of suits.

Our eyes locked briefly, before I looked away in embarrassment. I was ashamed for anyone to see me in the condition that I was in—especially him.

He stalled as if he wanted to say something—but I didn't give him a chance to as I rushed inside the penthouse and slammed the door behind me. Collapsing on my sofa, I buried my face in my hands and started crying.

"Why can't I just have some mothafucking peace?! Why is my life burdened with chaos and drama?! I just wanna be happy! I just wanna be happy and have a peace of mind!"

No more than two minutes into my pity party, there was a knock at my door. Peeling myself off the couch, I made my way to the front of the apartment to see who it was. Zane surely couldn't have gotten here that fast, unless he was right around the corner when he hit me, and I'd already told my girls that I needed some privacy after the altercation.

Needless to say, I was startled to find my neighbor standing outside of my door. "What do you want?" I asked, cautious and curiously.

He held up a first aid kit.

Without further questions, I stepped to the side and allowed him entrance. Bella, my cream and chocolate Bichon Frise, scurried over to sniff his shoes and I quickly shooed her away.

Normally, she was always guarded and leery of strangers, but for some reason, she was uncharacteristically affectionate with him. Bella wasn't even this friendly with Miracle and Chloè, and they came over all the time.

Embarrassed, and unusually quiet, I took a seat on the couch and watched him open the first aid kit. We locked eyes for a prolonged beat and then I looked away. There were no words exchanged between us as he gently cleaned my wounds with antiseptic.

The scent of his cologne was intoxicating, and before I knew it, I was lost in a trance, captivated by everything that made him who he was. His tall, muscular build, his caramel complexion, his dark bedroom eyes, his thick, juicy lips, the small scar that ran horizontally across the bridge of his nose, and most of all his mysteriousness.

Damn. What was it about him that made me crave him so badly?

The effect he had on me was puzzling. Hell, it was downright scary. No man in life ever had this strong of a hold on me—not even Zane.

"Why are you staring at me like that?" he asked. His warm, minty breath tickled my skin, causing my nipples to erect.

"No reason..." I lied. The close proximity made me suddenly turn bashful.

"Well, don't misread my kindness," he said. "I just couldn't ignore the state you were in…or the fact that you avoided a hospital."

"I didn't want to go to the hospital because I didn't want reports circulating about my ass whooping."

His eyebrows pointed up in an inquisitive fashion. "*Ass whooping?*" he repeated. "All that mouth you got, and you don't know how to defend yourself?"

"I grew up in Brentwood, surrounded by rich white people. I had no real reason to fight or defend myself," I told him. "Besides…none of that even matters. The media found out about the fight anyway…Now I'm the laughingstock of the world."

"You probably are."

I shot him a spiteful glare after he agreed with me.

"But the pain and ridicule won't last forever," he continued. "Take your L like a champ and keep it thuggin'. You're a rising star. I'm sure there's worse things you've conquered to get to where you are."

"You're right. I did. But I also ain't have to deal with bitches like Tika on the regular. I swear that broad has been out to get me since day one."

He held my eyes for a moment. "Well then, the battle she's fighting isn't with you. It's with herself. Don't give her the satisfaction of watching you suffer. My pops always told me success is the best revenge."

A smile crossed my lips as I allowed his words of wisdom to settle in. He was absolutely right. I couldn't let that bitch Tika get me down. My audition was in a few days and I planned on knocking that shit out of the park.

I wasn't some D-list actress, or the girlfriend of a music producer. I was Alaïa mothafucking Westbrook!

"Success is the best revenge," I repeated, loving the way it rolled off my tongue. No one had ever told me that before today, and I would never forget it. From here on out, it would be the quote that I solidly lived by. "Hey...You know what I just noticed?"

He placed a small Band-Aid on my chin, from where Tika had scratched me. "What's that?"

I smiled up at him shyly. "You actually do know who I am. All this time, I thought you didn't."

Without skipping a beat, he said, "Of course I know who you are. Do *you* know who you are?"

"I'm Alaïa mothafucking Westbrook," I gloated. "Now who are you? I don't even know your name, with your grumpy mothafucking ass."

He paused and tensed up slightly. "L," he simply said.

"*L*? Your name is L? Your mother just only named you a letter." My tone was laced with skepticism. I highly doubted that was his government, but he didn't argue with me, so I continued. "Well, okay, *Mr. L*, where are you from? Where'd you grow up?"

"I was born in Germany but I've traveled all over the world. My father was in the service, so we never stayed anywhere for too long. So, to answer your question, I can't say I'm from anywhere."

That satisfied my mild curiosity, and I filed that little tidbit away. As he treated my wounds, my eyes traveled to his thick lips. He was so complex. So sexy and enigmatic. His good looks, his deep voice, his obscure but charming appeal...There was a darkness and conflicted nature about him that I found rather interesting.

He didn't know where he was from, but I sure as hell knew where he was going. And that was with me...to the Oscars...as my man.

"There you go...staring at me like that again," he said uneasily.

There was a slight smile on his face, revealing one of his dimples. He was so handsome. So incredibly handsome and charismatic. His quiet mystique carried him, and his presence alone had me infatuated. Smitten by him.

Suddenly, without thinking, I leaned in to kiss him—and he quickly moved away, offended.

"That ass whooping must've left you delirious." He was taken aback, and it took him a few seconds to recover. "I already told you, you ain't my type of bitch."

Deflated and downright disappointed, I watched him close the first aid kit and stand to his feet.

"Goodnight...with your troublesome ass," he said on his way out the door, once again leaving me with a wounded pride and wet pussy.

11

L

On my way out of Alaïa's apartment, I ran smack into the nigga Zane. I recognized him almost immediately from our brief encounter at the club. What I didn't understand was why he was standing in my way. What type of fucking business did he have with Alaïa?

I know this clown ass nigga ain't her ex...

"Yo, what the fuck is this shit?" he yelled, looking from me to Alaïa.

His reaction gave me all the answers I needed.

Before either of us could respond, he snatched his gat out and pointed it at my head.

"Oh my God, Zane! WHAT THE FUCK ARE YOU DOING?!" Alaïa screamed, hopping off the couch.

"Did he beat?" Zane demanded to know.

"Nigga, have you lost your fucking mind! Put that fucking gun down—"

"Did he hit?!" Zane hollered.

"You're fucking crazy! Put the fucking gun down—"

As soon as he took his eyes off me, I easily disarmed him and pointed the pistol at his face. "How you like it, fuck nigga?" Grabbing him by the shirt, I slammed his ass against the wall, and pressed the gun to his crown. "How you like a gun pointed at yo shit? You gon' pull a mothafucking strap out on me, bitch? Do you know who the fuck I am?! Huh? You know who the fuck I am, nigga! My name good out here, fam!" Spit flew out my mouth as I yelled through clenched teeth. I turned into a maniac anytime I got a hold of a weapon. And I didn't take kindly to him putting a gun to my head. Mothafuckas got killed for less. This nigga had to be out his mothafucking mind fucking with me.

"L! Stop! Don't do it!" Alaïa pleaded, rushing to his defense. "What did you just tell me a minute ago? Be the bigger man and walk away. It's not worth it."

Eyes locked on Zane, I kept the pistol to his head and my finger on the trigger. "I'm already the bigger man," I told her.

Alaïa held her breath as she waited on me to make my move. There was enough tension in the room to slice a knife through. Even with the gun to his dome, Zane looked like he wanted to put hands on me. The nigga obviously wasn't afraid of the outcome. And if it hadn't been for

Alaïa standing there, begging me to spare him, shit definitely wouldn't have ended in his favor.

Swallowing my pride and resentment, I lowered the gun, removed the magazine, and tossed the useless weapon at his feet. "Next time you point a fucking gun at me, you better be prepared to use it." And with that, I left her apartment, showing mercy for the first time in my life. The nigga should've been on his knees, kissing Alaïa's fucking feet. If it hadn't been for her, I would've painted the mothafucking walls with that mothafucka's DNA. Once again, Alaïa had me breaking every rule in the book for her.

12

ZANE

As soon as the nigga left her crib, I directed my attention and anger at Alaïa. "Bitch, you got two seconds to tell me who the fuck that nigga is!" I demanded to know. "And why the fuck was he in this mufucka?! Is that why you been ducking me? 'Cuz you been running 'round the hood with that bum ass nigga?"

"And what if I am?" she challenged. "What's it to you? It ain't yo mothafucking business! I'm not yo bitch! I have every fucking right to replace yo monkey ass."

"Bitch, you can never replace a real nigga."

"*A real nigga?*" she laughed. "Since when did beating and cheating on your girl make you a real nigga?"

"Quit dancing 'round the question, bitch. Is you fucking that nigga or nah?"

Alaïa grimaced and folded her arms. "Maybe."

"Ho, don't fuck with me. I swear on life, if you fucking that nigga, both ya'll mothafucking asses gon' be in a mothafucking casket!"

"Why the fuck do you care what I do with my pussy?"

Grabbing her by the arm, I snatched her lil' ass towards me. "Bitch, this *my* mothafucking pussy," I told her. "I was the first nigga up in it and I'mma be the last nigga to come up out of it. I own this mufucka." The vice grip I had on her arm let her know that I wasn't playing. She still belonged to me. I didn't give a fuck if I was running 'round LA with some other ho. Alaïa would always be my bitch.

"Get the fuck off me, Zane! You're hurting my arm with them long ass coke nails! Get them nasty ass claws off me!"

She writhed in my embrace, but I refused to relinquish her. "Shut the fuck up. I ain't gon' ever let you go," I said, ignoring her complaints. "So nip that shit in the bud. 'Cuz I'll be damned if I share this good pussy—especially with some clown you met in the club."

"Back up off me, Z. You wanna find something to jump up and down in, go call that ho Tika. The day I left yo ass is the day you lost access to this good pussy."

"Man, fuck Tika. She ain't got that super-soaker like you. Only reason I'm fucking with that burnt-out bitch is to pass time. I don't give a fuck about that ho. None of these bitches mean shit to me. If the bitch wanted to end shit tomorrow, I wouldn't even lose sleep."

Alaïa rolled her eyes like she didn't believe me.

Cupping her chin, I forced her to look at me. "That's on God. Without you, a nigga feel empty. You my fucking life, Laï. I put in time with you. We got history. Mufucka can't walk away from that shit, bay. I can't just accept defeat. Fuck that. I refuse to let some other nigga have you. Yo ass belong to me. Shit, just thinking 'bout you with that other nigga got me feeling homicidal."

"Well, how you gon' do it without a weapon," she laughed. "You let him relieve you of your weapon in less than two seconds."

"Oh, bitch, you funny, huh." I tried to kiss her, but she mushed my face away.

"Move, Zane, seriously. I'm not trying to smell Tika's funky ass monkey."

"Man, I ain't never ate that bitch's muffin. Don't ever disrespect me. You the only one that get that type of treatment."

"Bullshit! That bitch tried to snatch my edges out! I doubt it was over a nigga that never ate her pussy. Who the fuck is you trying to fool, Zane? Me or yourself?"

"That's real. I reserve that special treatment for my queen. Speaking of which, it's been a minute since I had a taste," I said, backing her up against the wall.

"Well, you gon' stay parched, nigga, 'cuz it ain't fucking happening," Alaïa argued.

"Oh, it's already happening," I said, lowering myself at waist-level.

Before she could further argue, I pulled up her dress and stuffed my face in her juicy pussy. She wasn't wearing any panties underneath, so getting to it was rather easy.

"Zane, stop," she moaned, pushing and pulling my head at the same time.

Pulling her pearl between my lips, I licked and sucked on it vigorously, sliding my tongue in her slit every so often to sample her nectar. She began to moan as I moved my tongue in and out, thrusting her hips forward, and getting into the action. Her pussy was so good and fresh. I could tell she hadn't fucked that nigga prior to my arrival. Alaïa could say whatever the fuck she wanted, but this pussy was still mine. It would always be mine.

Groaning like a starved animal, I ran my tongue along her tight, sweet anus. Alaïa was lost in sensation as she held the top of my head, shivering against the wall, fighting with herself not to cum too soon. I knew how much she loved when I did that shit.

Holding her in place, I fucked her ass with the tip of my tongue, my nose buried deep into her pussy. The natural scent of her womanhood was intoxicating. She had my shit harder than $20 worth of jawbreakers. I was ready to break this dick off in her ass, but I wanted to get her right first. If I didn't, some other clown would.

Grabbing her ass cheeks, I pulled her closer and ran my tongue up and down the hood of her clitoris. It had been too long since I sucked on this juicy pussy. I sipped and slurped on her wetness, getting more than a mouthful of her sweet, sticky juices.

"Shit, Zane! Don't stop!" Her legs turned to jello as I peeled back the hood, and started tickling her clit with the tip of my tongue at rapid speed.

I took full control of her pleasure as I probed her hole deeper and deeper, licking in the hot, wet dampness of her vagina.

"Oh God!" she gasped, shivering from excitement. Her fingernails clawed into my scalp; she could barely handle the overwhelming sensation.

I stopped, looked up at her and smiled my most wicked smile as I watched her quiver in front of me. This pussy had my name written all over it. "Cum in my mouth," I said calmly. "I wanna taste everything you have to offer." Burying my face in her cunt, I munched on her pussy with enthusiasm, flicking my tongue across her clit like a seven-speed bullet.

"*Ooooooh*! I'm 'bout to cum!" she bellowed, pushing my face deep into her crotch.

I groaned, getting harder and harder by the second, my tongue flicking frantically across her juicy, little clit.

Shuddering, she closed her eyes, and releases her liquids all over my face and chin. Like a starving animal, I licked her clean, careful not to waste a single drop of her sweet nectar.

After wiping my wet mouth, I stood to my feet and reached for my belt. Now that I'd made her cum, I was ready to bend her ass over—but unfortunately, Alaïa had other plans.

"The fuck you think you're doing? You're done here," she told me, stumbling to the couch. "I got what I needed. You can let yourself out now."

Alaïa was straight savage, but I'd be lying if I said that shit didn't turn me on. "You not gon' act like that."

"Make sure to lock the door behind you."

Chuckling to myself, I shook my head in amusement. I wasn't tripping about her holding out on me. I had bitches, so it wasn't shit for a ho to get me off. Besides, sex wasn't my sole purpose for wanting Alaïa back. Even though she didn't believe me, I meant every single word that I'd said to her. She was my life; my soulmate. I had our whole future carved out for us.

"You dead ass wrong leaving a nigga stranded, but it's all good. I can knock that shit out at the crib."

Alaïa collapsed on her couch. "Yeah, I'm sure Tika's waiting for you, legs spread," she said, curling into a fetal position. Now that she'd gotten hers, she was ready for a nigga to bounce. From the hallway, I admired how peaceful she looked. I wasn't perfect by far, and Lord knows, I had my demons, but I truly wanted to do right by Alaïa. She was the only bitch that mattered to me. And no matter how bougie people said she acted, that was my bougie bitch.

"Aight then. I see you on yo bullshit. I'mma bounce," I told her. "But just know when you want this dick, I'mma make you beg for it."

"Goodnight, with your troublesome ass."

I shook my head at the utter disrespect. "You better remember what the fuck I said. Whatever you and that nigga got going on...end that shit, before I end it for you."

13

CHLOÈ

Seated at the sushi bar in *Nobu*, me and Miracle shared a tray of raw salmon and softshell crab rolls. I'd been staying with her the past few days, and her company really helped me cope with the loss of Bruce. It wasn't easy, but every day I grew a bit stronger and accepting of that fact that he was gone.

"Have you talked to your mom lately?" Miracle suddenly asked. She was attuned to my gloominess and sadness, and knew my mom had a lot to do with it.

"Girl, bye. I have nothing to say to that witch."

"You're gonna have to face her eventually."

"Yeah, well, I'm not rushing that moment. To be honest, I'm kind of enjoying the time apart. I get sick of her ass trying to control my pussy and my life. I'm just a meal ticket to that bitch. She doesn't even see me as a person, let alone her daughter. I'm tired of living that way, M."

"Maybe you should tell her that."

I gave Miracle a sidelong glare. "Is this your way of kicking me out?"

"Girl, stop. You can stay for as long as you want. That's not the problem," she said. "I just hate that you don't speak up for yourself when it comes to your mom. You say you're tired of her controlling your life, then put your fucking foot down. If you don't stand for something, you'll fall for anything."

"It's not that easy..." I mumbled.

"And why's that?"

"'Cuz apart of me feels obligated to take care of her. I mean, we're all we got at the end of the day. How else would she make it without me—"

"That's her problem, not yours!" Miracle argued. "If she wants to live the high life so bad, then let her go out and sell her pussy and asshole to the highest bidder. It's not your responsibility to take care of her."

"You're right."

"Look, Chloè. You're my ace, and I love you to death, and I'm only telling you this because I care about you. But you need to know...A person is only going to do what you allow them to. If you're tired of living that way, then you need to put your damn foot down. Plain and simple."

Miracle was only stating facts. I couldn't allow my mother to pimp me out for the rest of my life...but telling her that wasn't just so plain and simple. She wouldn't go for hearing that shit. Not after she gave up her singing career for me—which was something she loved to bring up any chance she got. With no husband and no job, my mother solely depended on me for financial support. It was a lot of responsibility for one person, but someone had to do it.

Heavy is the head that wears the crown, she'd always say.

"I'm gonna talk to her about it," I lied. Truthfully, I just wanted Miracle to drop the subject, because it only served to put me in a bad mood.

"I think you should," Miracle agreed.

All of a sudden, our waiter arrived and asked if we'd like to order our entrees. Before either of us could respond, a tall, handsome, suited man walked up and whispered something in his ear.

"Very well, sir," the waiter smiled. "I'll fetch that right away."

Miracle and I exchanged confused looks as the waiter scurried off to retrieve whatever the man had requested.

"Mind if I take a seat?" he asked, pulling the chair out next to me.

He was peanut butter brown with green eyes, short curly hair, and an award-winning smile. He reminded me of former NBA player Rick Fox, and he had the same suave appeal about himself.

If I had to guess, I'd say he was in his mid-to-late 30s, but judging from the silver in his hair and beard, he could've just as easily been older. Nevertheless, he was fine as fuck, and he smelled heavenly too.

"It's all yours," I told him.

"I like the sound of that," he winked. "What's your name, pretty?"

I blushed. "Chloè. And you?"

"Ahmad."

In an attempt to introduce herself, Miracle stuck out her hand for him to shake. "Hi. I'm Mir—"

"So," he said, ignoring her outstretched hand. "Tell me, queen. Are you single?"

Miracle surreptitiously ran her hand through her hair, trying to play off the embarrassment.

"Yes…" I told him. "I'm single."

"Well, as of today, consider yourself off the market."

I raised an eyebrow in skepticism. "Is that so?"

"A man has to seize the opportunity before someone else does. And it just so happens that I'm a man that knows what he wants."

"And what's that?"

"We can discuss the details over drinks," he said.

Speaking of drinks, the waiter returned with the most expensive bottle of champagne on the menu. After popping the cork, he poured us each a generous amount. "Have you lovely ladies finally made a decision on your entrees?"

"Yes. I'll have the lobster in truffle butter sauce," I ordered.

"And I'll have the ribeye," Miracle said.

Our guest signaled to the waiter that our bill was on him. Not only was he handsome, he was also generous. Me and Miracle's entrees were both over $70. "You really don't have to do that," I told him, playing it off.

"Oh, but I do. You see, I'm not the kind of man that lets my woman pay for anything. You keep your money, and let me take care of everything from here on out."

Something in his expression or tone of voice piqued me. "So that's the kind of man you are, huh?"

"That's the kind of man I am. What kind of woman are you—Wait. Don't tell me. I read somewhere that you can learn a lot about a person from a simple question."

I looked at him appraisingly. "Is that so?"

"What's one country you always wanted to visit?" There was a curious gleam in his eyes.

The question somewhat caught me off guard. "Um...I'll have to say Greece. What about you?"

He smiled and rubbed his beard. "Funny enough, the same place." Standing to his feet, he pulled out a business card. "Well, I don't wanna hold you up."

He handed me the card and I quickly read it over. Hovhannisyan Enterprises. A real estate company specializing in design, construction, and sales. I immediately recognized the Armenian surname. The man had billboards all throughout the city. In other words, I'd hit the mothafucking jackpot!

"Give me a ring tomorrow," he said. "I'd love to learn more about my future."

14

ALAÏA

"Hello. My name is Alaïa Marie Westbrook. I'm 22 and currently signed with Capital Entertainment. Some of my credits include Starlight, The Other Side of the Game, Falling for a Street Legend, and the Man with Many Talents—which won a Saturn and Sundance festival feature film award. It was also nominated for an Oscar," I beamed in pride. "For the role of 'Cameron', I plan to bring depth, freshness, and originality to the character."

Pulling out the script, I cleared my throat and prepared to read off the scene to the producer and casting director. There was a camera rolling in the background, but I was trained to tune it out.

"Silk! Why the fuck you be coming to my job on that bullshit? You know this is my place of business! How would you..." My voice trailed off as thoughts of Zane and L consumed me. Zane because of what happened between us and...well, L was always on my mind. Realizing how amateurish and unprofessional I looked, I cleared my throat and tried again. "Silk! Why the fuck you be coming to my job on that bullshit? You know this is my place of business! How would you feel if you came..." *Shit*! I silently cursed myself after fucking up the line. Stress and overwhelming emotions caused me to fumble my recitation. Both men were impacting my performance in the worst possible way. I should've never gotten mixed up with either one of those niggas. Clearing my throat once more, I attempted to read the script again. "Silk! Why the fuck you be coming to my job on that bullshit? You know this is my place of business. How would you feel if I came to your job while you was working and paid for some nigga to swing his dick in my face?" Sighing in frustration, I ran a hand through my curls. "I'm sorry. I'm sorry. I just wasn't feeling that one. Can I do it again?" I asked the producer.

"No need," the casting director said. "We'll call you if we're interested." There was finality in his tone, and I knew it was no point in arguing with him.

"Thank you for the opportunity and consideration."

After collecting my belongings, I left the building in tears. Miracle had worked so hard for me to get the role of Cameron, and I'd fucked it up in a matter of minutes. What the hell was wrong with me? Why did I sabotage my chances of being selected? I needed that credit, and now the opportunity was far beyond my reach.

Dammit, Alaïa! Way to fucking go!

Escorted by my security, I climbed into my tinted-out Escalade and slid my Gucci shades back on. I didn't want anyone to see me in the state that I was in. I was utterly disappointed in myself.

What the hell was I thinking?

How the fuck did I let myself screw up this badly?

I swear to God, I'm nothing but a fuck up!

Maybe the fans were right. Perhaps, my 15 minutes of fame had finally come to an end.

Tears rolled down my cheeks as the realization hit me. Distracted by thoughts of failure and misfortune, I didn't notice at the time that someone was following me.

15

CHLOÈ

That afternoon, I decided to finally hit up the affluent business owner I'd met at *Nobu*. I thought about playing it cool and hitting him in a month or so, but I figured it was no point in wasting time. Ahmad had chosen me out of all the beautiful women in LA, and I needed to seize the opportunity before it passed me by.

I met plenty niggas with money, but it wasn't every day that I crossed paths with wealthy entrepreneurs. Ahmad was a billionaire pioneer in real estate development. He might've been joking about the 'future' thing, but I had a plan to get a ring sooner or later—even if I had to fuck an engagement out of his ass.

I was tired of being pimped out by my mother, and I needed someone to help me get over Bruce. I wanted to be made wifey, so I'd never have to sell myself again, or come second to another woman. This ho life was for the birds. I needed a real nigga to pull up and make me into an honest woman before my pussy maxed out its mileage.

Hopefully, that man was Ahmad.

Ahmad's phone rang three times before his deep baritone filled the receiver. "Damn. I've been waiting on your ass," he answered.

"How do you know who this is?"

"What did I just say?"

I scoffed and shook my head.

"Where are you?" he asked.

"At my girl's crib. Why? Should I be somewhere else?"

"You should. Shoot me the address. I'mma send one of my drivers to come swoop you."

"Just like that?" I laughed.

"Let's skip the pleasantries. Life is short. I told you, I'm a man that knows what he wants. And what I want is to put a ring on your finger."

Blushing through the phone, I twirled one of my curls between my fingers. Ahmad was making this shit *too* easy. It was almost too good to be true. "I'll text you the address, and we'll talk more about this later."

After hanging up, I rushed to put on the sexiest dress I could find and paired it with some pink So Kates. Miracle curled my hair—since her shit was always laid—and I did my makeup minimally.

An hour later, the private driver that Ahmad sent arrived. I felt so pampered climbing into the Maybach. Waiting for me in the backseat was a small black bag from Vintage Malibu's jewelry store. Allowing my curiosity to roam, I grabbed the bag, peeked inside, and spotted a small velvet jewelry box.

Oh my God!

Did this nigga really do what I think he did?

With trembling fingers, I pulled out the box and lifted the lid in excitement. My lips parted with a sharp intake of breath and my eyes bulged. Inside the satin slit was a sparkling 16-carat engagement ring.

As if on cue, my phone vibrated with a text. It was from Ahmad and read:

If you don't like it, I'll let you pick out something better ;)

Is this nigga serious, I asked myself?

Where are you, I texted back.

No response.

Thirty minutes later, I arrived at a private landing strip in Camp Creek, Georgia, near the airport. The private driver pulled into the gated lot with an access card and took me to a Boeing jet that Ahmad was standing next to.

What the hot sauce in my bag? Why the hell did this nigga bring me to the airport?

After parking, the chauffeur hopped out and opened the back door. Ahmad took my hand and helped me out of the vehicle. "Why am I here?" I asked him. "What other tricks do you have up your sleeve?"

"You got the ring. I already laid all my cards on the table."

"I thought you said you wanted to get to know more about me," I reminded him.

"And I will. On this 18-hour flight to Mykonos."

My smile broadened into satisfaction and overwhelming joy. He was taking me to Greece! Right now—today! I felt like I was in a dream! Men had showered me with gifts and endless cash, but none of them took me halfway around the world. Speechless, I allowed him to lead me up the stairs to the aircraft. I didn't know a damn thing about Ahmad, but something about him made me want to throw caution to the wind.

Fuck it.

Life *is* short.

16

MIRACLE

ONE WEEK LATER

That afternoon, me and the girls got together at *Nail Bar and Beauty Lounge* in Beverly Hills. We were all overdue for manis and pedis, and we needed to fill each other in on the latest happenings of our lives.

As usual, Alaïa had to start with her own bullshit, since she thought the world revolved around her.

"Y'all will not believe the dumb shit I did yesterday." She had her puppy in her lap, getting its nails polished. Alaïa really went all out for that damn dog. You would've thought the bitch was her fucking baby.

"First, tell us how the audition went, bitch. I been waiting on pins and needles."

She frowned. "Bitch, I ain't get that shit."

I immediately choked on the bottled water I was sipping. "Damn, bitch! Are you serious?! The only reason I ain't ask about it was because I knew you'd sealed the deal! How the hell did you fuck up that audition? You knew how important it was!"

"And so did you! Why weren't you there to support me?" Alaïa questioned.

"Bitch, I was in a meeting with a potential client of yours, kissing ass and licking balls to get you that MAC endorsement you wanted so bad! So don't talk to me about support! I been A-1 since day one!"

Alaïa tossed her hands up in surrender. "You right. That's my bad."

I waved her off in forgiveness. "You good, boo. Forget about it. There's plenty other roles out there with your name on it," I encouraged. Of our trio, I was always the positive and optimistic one.

"You'll get it next time, babe," Chloè told her.

"So what's the dumb shit you did?" I asked. Now that she'd told me about the audition, I figured nothing could be worse.

"I fucked around and let Z eat the box."

Scratch that! Shit could be much worse.

"Bitch, did you fall and bump your head? Have you really forgotten the way he used to beat your ass and cheat on you? Do you really wanna go back to that shit?!" Chloè berated.

"I didn't say I wanted to go back. I just said he ate the box."

"And how the fuck did that happen?"

"To be honest...I don't know. One minute we were arguing, the next he was chowing on my muffin. I'm not sure how it happened. I just know that it happened."

"So, if Tika get at that ass again—."

"That bitch can fuck around and see round 2 if she want to. I ain't scared of that ho. 'Cuz you know I'll beef up on security."

I rolled my eyes. Alaïa always talked big shit till it came time to throw hands. Luckily, she had niggas on her payroll to do the dirty work for her. "*Anyway*...what's new with you, Chloè?" I asked, wanting to shift focuses. Alaïa could be so self-absorbed, and if I didn't stop her early, she would only go on and on. "Yo ass been MIA these last few days, ignoring my calls like I was a fucking bill collector. Wassup with that?"

Chloè smiled and blushed. "I was out of town."

"With who? G Money?"

G Money was her second-favorite trick after Bruce. He kept her in all the hot designer shit, and bought her a Benz for her 25th birthday. Bruce got jealous though, and made her give that shit back. G Money was a Compton rapper, who was signed to the same label as Zane. He often produced tracks for him, and the niggas were thick as thieves. As a matter of fact, it was Zane who introduced them at his album release party.

"Bitch, bye! Me and that nigga G Money are history. Ever since the nigga had a baby on me, he's been acting like I'm non-important. So, I've been acting like he's non-existent. I ain't got time for nobody that ain't got time for me," she said. "Besides, I got a new nigga I been feeling. Fine ass mothafucka too...you remember homeboy from Nobu," she reminded me.

"Girl, shut up! You were out of town with him?"

"Flew my ass to Greece, I swear to God, girl."

"And what did ya'll mothafuckas do in Greece?" I asked, ears wide open.

"Sight-seeing, shopping, fine dining, and lots and lots of time spent together at the ocean. Girl, we had this nice ass beachside villa with floor-to-ceiling windows and plushed out furniture. Every day chefs came to the villa to prepare our meals. Fresh fish, Moussaka, authentic gyro sandwiches, and the most delicious wine you've ever tasted! Not that cheap shit! I kid you not, it was the most romantic thing I've ever experienced. And believe you me, plenty niggas have romanced me out of my draws...But none of them niggas is fucking with Ahmad."

"So..." Alaïa said. "Has he romanced you out of *your* draws?" Her eyebrow was pointed up as she gave Chloè a knowing look.

"That's the thing. We haven't even fucked yet—nor has he made an effort to."

"*Hmm*. Be careful with that one, bitch. Remember, everything that glitters ain't gold," I told her.

Chloè became offended. "So just 'cuz the nigga ain't smack yet, I'm supposed to be on guard?"

"At least you know what to expect from the niggas who *do* wanna smash. You know what their motives are. Who knows what the fuck this nigga is on. I ain't hating or nothing, but dude just comes off as suspicious, low-key. The way he came at you in the restaurant. The way he flying you all over the world...Something's just off about him. I can't put my finger on it, but I don't trust homeboy...There's just something about him."

"You claim you ain't a hater, but your words say otherwise. Why can't you just be happy for me? If it were you, I'd be all for it. But since it ain't, you gotta play me like homeboy suspicious. Nah, bitch, it's *you* that's suspicious. Are you a friend or a foe? Bitch, pick a side. You can't straddle the fence."

"Really, bitch? *Really*? Yo mama put you out on yo ass, and I happily opened my home to you! Any time you needed a friend, I was there for you and now you wanna question my loyalty? I'm offended that you even trying me right now. And all over some clown who you just met. You don't know that nigga from Adam! All I said was homie seems fishy! You can take it how you wanna, but that's just how I feel. I don't know why you making a big deal about it anyway. All them niggas you fuck with be weird as shit."

"And this is coming from a bitch that has to tape her cock down. Ho, you the last mothafucka to be calling somebody weird."

Jumping to my feet, I tossed the bottled water at her, getting the liquid all over her and Alaïa. "Fuck you, bitch! You gon' act funny over a piece of dick! These niggas come a dime of dozen, ho! You better act like you know who's really there for you! These niggas may break you off every now and then, but it's yo girls who got yo back! One day, when all your bridges burn, you gon' realize that shit!"

"Bitch, I can't believe you got this water all over me," Chloè said, cleaning off her shirt. "You better get the fuck on 'fore I slap the shit outta you, Marcus. You got me madder than a bitch right now."

"SLAP ME, HO!" I tried to run up on her, but Alaïa jumped between us. "That's a straight shit eater move, ho! I dare you to say that to my fucking face!" I hated when anyone called me by my government name.

"Hey—hold up! What the hell are ya'll bitches doing? We family! Family don't squabble—especially over dick. Miracle's right. These niggas come a dime a dozen. You hoes need to chill. Ya'll acting a hot, hood ass mess. Let's just sit back, relax, and soak our feet. Shit ain't that serious. Now kiss and make up."

Leave it to Alaïa to play referee.

Swallowing her pride, Chloè turned to me and apologized. "I'm sorry, M. I was way outta line."

"You damn sure were...but all's forgiven, boo."

Chloè and Alaïa took their seats, and dipped their feet back into their bowls. The technicians were looking at us like we were crazy, but it was nothing they hadn't witnessed before. "I'll be back. I need to use the restroom." Honestly, I needed time to regroup, because Chloè had me hot than a mothafucka.

Excusing myself, I slipped into the bathroom and pulled out my cellphone. Zane's line rang several times, before he finally picked up. "The fuck do you want?" he asked, mildly irritated.

"You." I didn't even beat around the bush with it. I wanted to make my intentions crystal clear.

"Man, I'm in the studio right. If it ain't money-related, don't hit me—"

"So you and Alaïa trying to get that old thing back? Since when did ya'll start fucking with each other again?"

"Since when is it any of yo mothafucking business, bitch?"

"I waited for you to drop Alaïa, only for you to pick up Tika along the way. Now you back fucking with Alaïa again. When the fuck is you gon' realize these hoes don't love you like I love you! I been down for you from the beginning, Z! How the fuck is you gon'…" My voice trailed off as someone entered the restroom. Lowering my voice, I continued with my rant. "How the fuck is you gon' act like I ain't been real from the start?!"

"Bitch, I don't owe you shit—I don't even owe you an explanation! We ain't fucking no more. You ain't my bitch. You gon' have to get over it, sweetie! Expectations can get a mufucka killed."

My emotions threatened to choke me up. "Nigga, you already killing me," I cried. "You're killing me right now with your cold and ruthless ways. I will never understand how you can treat a person like shit that did so much for you. Nigga, you poppin' because of me!" I yelled. "If it weren't for me and my brothers robbing that stash house, you'd be still in Inglewood in that basement ass studio, making mothafucking beats for features! Nigga, *I* was there for you! Not Tika! Not Alaïa! Me—"

Click.

Zane hung the phone up on my ass, letting me know that I was the only one still fighting for us. He'd given up on me long ago, but I was the only one who couldn't move on with my life. As much as it hurt to admit, sometimes the hardest part of holding on is letting go.

***

After parting ways with Alaïa and Chloè, I hopped on the 110 free-way, and headed straight to the hood. I had to holla at my brothers about some business, and what I had to say warranted a face-to-face visit.

Thirty minutes later, I arrived at my grand mama's home on Grape Street in Compton. My brothers had moved in with her after our mother died, while I relocated to Hollywood to chase my dreams of stardom. Growing up, me and my brothers never got along, because they refused to accept my sexuality. But over the years, they learned to put up with and respect my way of life. Besides, I put money in their pockets on several occasions, helping them hit licks on ballers and rich Armenian businessmen.

I used to be on that street shit heavy before the entertainment industry took hold of me. Now I made an honest living as the publicist of my best friend. If not for meeting Alaïa in college, I would still be in the hood, hitting licks on corner boys. Fortunately for me, her parents took me in and paid for my education.

Even though, I didn't get as far as Alaïa in my career, I owed her everything for at least giving me a fair shot at it. It was because of her that I graduated from film school in the first place. I was thankful for everything she'd done, but I just couldn't stop myself from secretly envying her as well.

Her life and her lover should've been mine!

I was crazy about that nigga Zane; so much so that it drove me insane whenever I thought about him being with someone else. When I saw him at the club with Tika the other week, I wanted to claw that bitch's eyes out of her fucking head. I'd been patient for far too long! Now it was time for me to remind his black ass who the fuck I was. Nobody played Miracle and got away with the shit! The nigga needed to know what the hell I was capable of, because apparently, he'd underestimated me.

"Wus good, M?" Marlon greeted, puffing on a blunt. He was in an all blue jersey and blue snapback. At 27, he was the oldest and a known savage in the streets. "Long time, no see. What brought yo bougie ass to the hood?"

"Business."

"Type of business?" MiKel asked. He was the middle sibling, and a blood by association. Even though he and Marlon were brothers, they were ironically in separate gangs. And feuding sets at that. I didn't get it, but as long as they weren't shooting at each other, I didn't give a fuck.

"I got a lick for ya'll. And I'm talking big money."

Marlon rubbed his hands together mischievously. *"Big money, huh*? You must be ready to finally make that move on Alaïa."

"Hell no! I would never rob my home girl. Shit, as long as she eats, I eat. Why would I fuck up my meal ticket?"

"Ya plate would be even fuller if you stopped hanging onto that bitch's coattail. Should've cut the strings on that ho right after graduation. The bitch ain't been doing shit but holding you back, fam," Marlon said. "You oughta be hitting her mufuckin' pockets! You ain't shit to that ho but a charity case anyway! She only wants you around to feel indebted to her. That's why she never put you on, and that's real. Think about that shit."

"That's facts. You should'a been ganked that bitch," MiKel sided. "Then after we hit her ass, we should gank her mufuckin' folks. Everybody know they some millionaires. Yo ass sittin' on the *real* lick and you bullshitting. Choosing commitment over common sense. These streets don't know loyalty. It's all about getting that bag at the end of the day. Fuck a friendship."

Suddenly, I felt torn inside. Initially, I planned to have my brothers pull up on Zane, but after hearing what they had to say, I was now thinking about sending my goons after Alaïa. My brothers were right. I could get a lot more out of that egotistical bitch by just setting her ass up.

17

ZANE

After leaving the studio, I went to *The Grove* and stopped inside a couple stores to grab something special for my baby. She'd been giving a nigga the cold-treatment, so I had to go all out to get on her good side.

After running up a check, I headed back to the crib with bags from Coach, Barney's, Michael Kors, and Victoria's Secret. When I walked in the place, Tika automatically assumed they were for her.

"Aww, baby, you shouldn't have," she said, reaching for the bags.

I side-stepped her. "Trust me, bitch, I didn't."

"Well then, if they ain't for me, who the fuck are they for?" She hounded, following me through the house.

Walking past plaques and photos of me with Dre. Dre, Snoop, and Nipsey, I headed to the bedroom with Tika hot on my heels. "Answer me, Z! Who the fuck are they for?"

"Don't worry 'bout who they for. Just get'cho shit and get the fuck up outta here. Yo lease is up."

"Excuse me?" Tika was beyond offended. "Nigga, you must be gone off that Molly! I know you ain't putting me out my own mothafucking crib!"

"*Yo crib?* Bitch, yo name ain't on the lease nowhere. You just a tenant, paying in pussy. You knew what the fuck this shit was."

"What the fuck is you on? Where's all this coming from?"

"Bitch, I hate repeating myself. Stop running yo mouth and start using them hands."

"Nigga, I'm not finna pack up shit till you tell me what the fuck is wrong! What did I do? Why are you acting this way? At the very least, you owe me that much!"

"Bitch, I don't owe you shit! That's yo problem! You do too much! And you expect way too fucking much! I'm not looking for a relationship with your ass—nor do I plan on faking like I'm in one!"

"So why'd you move me in this bitch? Why let paparazzi take photos of us? Why—"

"Hol' up, bitch. Let's get one thing straight. You moved in this bitch and started hanging in the spotlight. No one told you to do that shit. We not in no mufuckin' relationship, so let's not act like we are. The first day we met, I smashed, so you knew what it was. You gotta get over it, sweetie. It was just sex," I said indignantly.

"What the fuck you mean it was just sex? Nigga, I been loyal to you from the start!" she cried. "Real ones don't get ran up in and ran off on!"

"Bitch, you wanted to be ran in!" I yelled. "And you being real disrespectful right now! Respect me as a man and stop fronting. I done asked you nicely to pack ya shit and get the fuck out. Don't make me get violent in this mufucka!"

"Well, nigga that's what the fuck you gone have to do cuz I ain't leaving this bitch without a fight!"

WHAP!

I slapped the shit out her dumb ass. If it was a mothafucking fight she wanted, it was mothafucking fight she would get.

"What the fuck, Z? Have you lost yo fucking mind?!" she screamed.

"Nah, but you 'bout to lose them teeth if you don't get the fuck up out my crib."

"You dirty dick, bitch! That's how you wanna play? Fine, then! Two can play that game!

I got something for that ass, nigga. I can't wait to run to the mothafucking blogs! They gon' all hear about yo coked out ass, and how you love for me to wear a strap-on—"

Stricken by rage, I started raining blows on her face and body. "YOU AIN'T GONE RESPECT ME AS A MAN! THEN I'MA BEAT YO ASS LIKE YOU A MOTHAFUCKING MAN!" Stomping her all in her chest and back, I whooped her ass like she was a nigga out in the streets.

Tika was leaking blood by the time I finally tired myself out. Bitch had to be out her mind, coming at me like she was crazy. I had to beat the fuck out a bitch, talking sideways to a nigga.

Grabbing her by the hair, I dragged her bloodied, battered body through the mansion and tossed her out on her ass. I wouldn't even let her get her shit before leaving. She'd already lost that privilege, running her mothafucking mouth. For all I cared, that expensive shit could go in the mothafucking dumpster on Skid Row. I just wanted this bitch out of my sight. Fighting Alaïa behind my back was one thing, but disrespecting me was a whole other.

"Yo time is up," I told her. "Now get the fuck off my property before you really see a nigga's bad side."

Tika scrambled to her feet and backed off. "You gon' pay for this shit!" she threatened. "I can guaran-damn-tee you that!" Climbing in her car, she started the engine and rolled her window down. "On everything, you gone pay for this shit, bitch!" She spat a mouthful of blood at my Ferragamo slippers, then peeled off with her middle finger up in the air.

Fuck that burnt-out bitch, I told myself.

After cleaning out all of Tika's shit, I tidied up the place and restored it to its original bachelor state. That way, if Alaïa came over, she'd see that no other bitches had taken her place. I may've been fucked up, but my heart was in the right place and, despite our rocky past, I harbored hope for our future. But before I could take that next step with Alaïa, I needed to find out more about that bitch ass neighbor of hers.

I didn't like running onto the battlefield blindly. To win a war, you first had to know how the enemy strategized. And once, I found out everything I needed to, I'd eliminate that mothafucka from the equation, once and for all.

18

ALAÏA

I was on my way back home when Miracle suddenly hit me up out of the blue. Seeing her number on my screen was somewhat of a surprise, considering the fact that I'd just seen her a couple hours ago. What did she have to tell me that she couldn't have told me earlier?

Pressing the green button, I placed the phone to my ear. "Hey, wassup, girl?"

"I got good news, *biiiitch*!" she sang jovially.

"Bitch, I could use some good news. Tell me."

"I just got a call from the casting director for *Cameron*. He said his first option didn't fall through, so he's choosing you for the star role!" Miracle squealed in delight. "Isn't that great? You got the part!"

"I don't want it," I pouted.

"Excuse me, bitch? Did you not just hear what the fuck I said. You got the lead mothafucking role!"

"I don't care. I don't want it if I didn't get it on my own merit. The role was only given to me 'cuz Zendaya is shooting another movie. I'm not stupid. I know what's up."

"Who gives a fuck? The role is yours now. That's all that matters. Quit being prideful and be thankful. The competition was pretty steep for that gig. And from what I heard, your audition wasn't the best. And if you think about it, you did get the role based on your merit. It was your credits and past performances that ultimately sealed the deal."

Smiling arrogantly, I happily agreed. "You're right. I got that role 'cuz they know I'm that bitch."

"Congrats, boo. We need to celebrate tomorrow! And I got the perfect place in mind too! Keep yo phone on you, boo, I'mma shoot you the details in an hour or so."

"Alright. Will do. And thanks, a lot, Miracle. I couldn't have done it without you."

There was a brief pause on her end. "You're my ace, bitch. I love you to death."

"I love you too, M. Talk to you later."

After hanging up with Miracle, I screamed in triumph. I was in my topless Audi A5 with the wind blowing through my curls. Normally, I had security chauffeur me around the city, but that day, I decided to do my own thing. I felt free, independent, untouchable, and victorious.

Won't He do it!

Earlier on the phone, I was bullshitting to keep up my façade, but truthfully, I was relieved to get the lead role that would undoubtedly put me on the map. Everybody would know Alaïa Westbrook. When it was all said and done, I was sure to be a household name.

***

Twenty minutes later, I arrived at my apartment building and pulled into the covered parking garage. After easing into my designated spot, I put the top up, and turned off the car. Grabbing Bella, I climbed out, and hit the car lock on my key ring. As I headed towards the elevator, I gushed over Bella's new haircut.

Every month, I spent close to 5 grand, just in her upkeep and grooming. I didn't mind the extra bill, because I loved my dog like she was my own child. "Bella, you swaggin' on these bitches now—"

WHAP!

Bella fell from my hands after something hard and heavy struck me. The impact of the blow sent me spiraling to the ground, where I landed right next to Bella. She scurried away in fear as my attacker loomed over me.

"What the fuck?"

I tasted blood in my mouth from where I accidentally bit my tongue, and I was certain that I had a concussion. I'd never hit been hit so hard in all my life. Grabbing my head, I looked up at my attacker. He was a tall, burly mothafucka with braids and bad acne.

"I'm sorry that we had to meet this way. But it was my only means of getting you alone."

"Why did you—who are you?" I didn't recognize him immediately, but that could've been attributed to my concussion. "Why the fuck did you hit me? What the fuck do you want? Money?!"

He smiled. "It's not about what I want. It's about what I want to give."

My eyes darted between him and the elevator as he continued talking. Apart of me felt like making a run for it, but I was positive that I wouldn't get very far.

"Perhaps, you don't remember," he said. "I'm the one who sent that sweet, little letter to you some months back. It was pretty self-explanatory, and stated every single thing I had planned for when I finally got you alone."

I quickly realized he was my stalker and reached for the gun in my purse. Before I could grab my shit, he kicked the hell out of me, knocking the wind from my chest.

"Do you remember what I said, bitch?"

He kicked the shit out of me again, causing my sunglasses to fly off.

"I told ya ass I'd catch you slipping!"

"SOMEBODY HEL—"

Climbing on top of me, he started wailing on my ass like I was a nigga that was twice his size. Every time, he hit me my skull bounced off the ground. I was sure that I'd need reconstructive surgery by the time he finished with my ass.

"You bougie bitch, you think you better than the rest of society?!" he yelled. "Let's see how high and mighty you are with this nut in yo gut!" Standing to his feet, he unbuckled his cheap, leather belt.

He barely had a chance to undo the strap before someone ran up and clocked his ass from behind. With blurred, double vision, I watched the fight ensue between L and my attacker. The stalker was twice his size, but L held his own like a mothafucking savage.

He must've knew how to box, because he managed to land an impressive punch that knocked the burly man off his feet. After dropping his ass, L snatched off his cheap belt and started beating him all over his body with it.

When that wasn't enough to satisfy him, he resorted to stomping his head into the concrete till his face caved in. His nose and mouth exploded with blood. He kicked his left eye out of his fucking skull as he stomped his ass repeatedly.

Completely devoid of a soul or conscious, L beat him within an inch of his life and didn't stop until the man had finally ceased all movement. I figured that he must've knocked him out cold...but to be honest, I wasn't really sure. He could've just as easily killed him.

With maniacal determination, L dragged him across the parking lot to his car. Obviously still alive, the man choked and wheezed due to the belt around his throat. His eye was dangling by a single chord of muscle, and he was gruesome to look at. From a safe distance, I watched L toss him into his trunk before slamming the lid shut.

Sore and stunned beyond a reasonable doubt, I was unable to stand on my own two feet. Rather fearful of L now, I tensed up as he approached me and scooped me up into his arms. Ignoring my rigidness, he carried me into the building.

He didn't say a single word as he lugged me into his unit and placed me on the sofa. "You are something fucking else, man. Who told you it was safe to wander without protection. You know better than to move around, unguarded," he said in a scolding tone. "You must have a fucking death wish or some shit."

There was a calm contentment about him as he fetched his first aid kit. I would never understand how he could beat a man to near death, then act like nothing ever happened. "I'll treat these wounds, but I really think you should see a doctor 'bout that knot on ya head. You took a hard hit there, and it might cause long-term damage."

"I can't go to the hospital," I argued. "I don't want this shit to get out to the media. I just got the role for Cameron, and I don't want this to damage my rep. Lord knows, I've been in the news enough in this past month alone! If one more story covers me, I think I'll lose it."

L continued to dress my face. "I won't press the issue."

"Thanks. I appreciate it." There was a long, awkward silence between us before I finally asked the inevitable. "What are you gonna do with that fucker? The nigga just came out of nowhere and attacked me. I'd be a fool not to put the prosecutor on that ass. It was because of him that I moved here in the first place. I have to make sure he doesn't do this shit to me or anyone else, ever again!"

"Don't worry," L told me. "Just get some rest. I'll take care of it." He should've been wilting with exhaustion after that tussle in the parking lot, but instead he was determined to carry on. He was such a huge solace to me.

"L!" I called after him. "Please find my dog. She's out there all alone."

He stood to his feet and walked out of the apartment, leaving me with the impression that he was going to the police. Little did I know, he had something much worse in store.

19

L

I dragged Alaïa's stalker through the warehouse on the outskirts of the city. In the basement, I had 50-gallon barrels that were filled with sulfuric acid. Anytime I needed to get rid of some shit fast, I would dispose of it in a way that made it possible for the law to find—and that's exactly what I planned to do with this ho ass mufucka.

"Why the fuck is you doing this, man?" he cried. "I wasn't gon' kill the bitch! I just wanted to scare her, man! I promise! Please! Please let me go!"

The smell of rotting flesh surrounded us as I dragged him to the back of the warehouse. Dozens of bodies were disposed of here, and the smell was practically embedded in the structure of the building. The entire place reeked of decomposition. I only used the warehouse to cover my tracks.

"Please, man, don't kill me! I got a family! I got kids! Please let me live! C'mon, please, man! I just a had a baby! C'mon, man! This shit ain't gotta end like this!"

"Bitch...this is the end."

POP!

With no remorse, I blew his brains out the back of his mothafucking head. As I continued to lug him to the basement, I started to smell a foul stench. The mothafucka had runny stool, oozing down his legs like piss, making my clean-up job *that* much harder.

Facing the daunting task with resignation, I cursed Alaïa in my head.

All the shit I do for this bitch, her ass should be down here with me.

I don't know why I shouldered the responsibility of her safety. I wasn't her nigga, but I made it my mission to protect her like I was.

20

CHLOÈ

Today was my first day back at home since my mother put me out over a week ago. We hadn't talked, but we texted a couple times, and I filled her in on everything that'd happened thus far; meeting Ahmad, the trip to Greece, and the proposal that I held back from telling my girls.

I didn't want them judging me for telling the man 'yes', because this was my life and not theirs, and I had to do what was best for me. After hearing that I landed another rich nigga, my mother happily welcomed me home with open arms and a warm embrace.

"Alright. Always keep in mind what I told you. All work and no play. We gotta keep this paper coming in," she said. "All work and no play keeps the shut-off notices away."

To celebrate the news, my mother hired an entire catering team to prepare a seafood feast. As she ran around the kitchen, directing orders at the chefs, I walked through the home and savored the warmth and familiarity of it.

I'd been fucking with Bruce for 10+ years, and never once came close to getting a ring. But I knew Ahmad for less than 24 hours, before he suddenly popped the question to me. It took him two weeks of concerted effort to achieve what Bruce never could.

The shit was surreal. All the years of hoeing finally paid off. I finally caught the break that I needed.

Stopping at an accent table, I grabbed the picture frame on top and admired the photo of my mother and her identical twin sister, Cathie. She'd died from an overdose in her early 20s, before I ever had the chance to get to know her.

My mother didn't talk much about her, and after a while, I began to forget she ever existed. The only thing we owned of remembrance was a black and white photo of them in their pre-teens.

As soon as I placed the photo down, my cellphone started ringing. Much to my dismay, it was the last person I wanted to hear from. "What the fuck do you want, Zane?"

"Come outside and find out."

I hadn't even been home an hour, and drama was already knocking on my front door. Slipping my feet into a pair of Gucci slide-ons, I left the house and found Zane leaning up against his Wraith out front.

"You got Tika and yo harem of hoes," I reminded him. "What the fuck could you possibly want with me?"

"I want you to tell me 'bout that nigga Laï been kicking shit with. The one I had to check in the club the other week."

"*Hmph.* That ain't how I recall it."

"Don't be funny, bitch."

"You the only funny bitch I see. You *here*, at *my* house, asking *me* 'bout another bitch. If you wanna know who the nigga is so bad, then pull his street cred! And why you care so bad what the fuck Alaïa does anyway! So what if she likes the nigga? You got a flock of bitches, with Miracle front and center!"

Zane shot me an evil glare.

"I walked in on her talking to you the other day. Yeah, nigga, I know."

He recovered smoothly from the surprise. "Bitch, keep yo mouth mothafucking closed."

"Nigga, my concern ain't who you fucking! Only thing I care about is Alaïa and making sure she aight! She deserves happiness with somebody that ain't gon' treat her like shit. So stop hating on a bitch, and let my girl live her mothafucking life."

"Bitch, don't stand here and front, 'cuz it wasn't that long ago you were sucking my dick for a stack. That bitch may think you a rider, but you just a wolf in sheep's clothing."

21

ZANE

I was leaving Chloè's crib when I got a call from my informant. Alaïa's home-girls weren't the only ones I was shaking down about that nigga, I had my folk pulling all types of papers to find out more shit on the mothafucka that lived next door to Alaïa.

"I hope you got good news," I answered.

"I wouldn't have called if I didn't," she said. My informant was a chick I used to fuck with, who worked down at the courthouse. She had all types of connects, and could get me any legal document that I needed.

"Wus good on it?"

"The cars, clubs, and condo he owns are all in separate names. There's no birth records on him, and his social-security number is a fake. Other than the documents on his home, clubs, and cars, he has no real paper trail to follow. But what I find most interesting is that all of the possessions are in a woman's name..."

Hearing that shit took me by surprise.

So, he has a bitch holding shit down for him, I thought.

An evil grin crossed my lips.

Now that I knew a bit more about him, I felt like I had the upper-hand.

"So when I'mma see you—"

I hung the phone up on her ass, without so much as a thank you. I didn't have time to entertain that ho. I was finally ready to put my plan into motion.

23

ALAÏA

An hour later, I woke up in an unrecognizable place. The room was empty, echoing, and cool. It took my brain several seconds to register that I was inside of L's apartment. He had all of the curtains drawn, and the AC on full blast.

Climbing off the sofa, I padded over to the temperature control system and powered it off. The inside of his place felt like Antarctica. Did he live like this every day? Pulling back the curtains, I let in some natural light from the city's skyline. Now his crib didn't feel like a mothafucking dungeon.

What type of person could live like that, I asked myself? *Cold and in the dark all the time.*

Looking myself over in the living room mirror, I almost didn't know who was staring back at me. I was so busy trying to figure out L, that I almost didn't recognize myself. That fat piece of shit really did a number on me. Lucky for me, filming for Cameron didn't start until this summer—which meant I had enough time to nurse myself back to health.

No matter what I do, I always attract drama...even when I'm minding my own damn business.

Taking my mind off the maniac in the parking lot, I wandered through L's place, bemusedly admiring his simple but sophisticated set-up. He didn't have a whole lot of electronics and technology. Just a small television in the living room—with basic cable—surrounded by a bookshelf with enough reads to make a library. The man obviously loved his books.

Walking over to the shelf on the left, I admired his collection, and tried to get a feel for his taste. He had every book by Robert Greene and Donald Goines. For some reason, *"The 33 Strategies of War"* caught my attention, and when I grabbed the book, it activated a lever that opened up the wall.

Frozen in shock, my lips parted with a sharp intake of breath. Revealed to be inside was a myriad of guns and grenades. Partly puzzled and partly vexed, I questioned why L had enough artillery for Word War 3. Why did he need so many weapons? Who the fuck was this nigga, and was I safe with him living next door to me?

All of a sudden, I heard the key turn in the door. Placing the book back on the shelf, the wall closed up, and I tried my best not to look so suspicious.

L walked in with a different set of clothes on, and a worry-free look, in spite of everything that happened. Bella was in his arms without a care in the world. "What the fuck is you doing?" he asked. "Looking for more shit to get into?"

He was in a much better mood after our last emotionally-charged encounter. "I was admiring your chess table," I lied, wanting to keep him in his good mood.

After putting down Bella, he pinned me with a shrewd glance. "You play?"

"Question is...do *you* play?"

Without another word, L started setting up the board. He and I took our respectful seats, and the competition was soon underway. "You know...My father was an avid chess player," he began. "He'd always say if I brought a woman home who couldn't play chess, he wouldn't like her. He was big on strategy, and didn't respect anyone that couldn't strategize."

Three games in, I had him re-thinking his own strategies, since I put him to shame in every round. "I think your dad would've liked me."

L didn't respond. But any sign of kindness coming from him would be odd.

I sensed his troubled mood, but I still felt confident enough to ask him about the guns. I was, however, a bit afraid of him to find out that I was snooping. I was never supposed to see those weapons, but now that I did, I wanted to know his reason for keeping them.

Who the fuck was this nigga? Why the hell did he need so many guns? And why on Earth was he hiding them?

There were a dozen thoughts churning through my mind at the same time. I prayed this mothafucka wasn't some deranged ass lunatic, but in today's world, you could never be too sure. "What'd you do with that guy that attacked me?"

He didn't spare me a glance as he continued to ogle the chess board. "I told you. I took care of it." He was measured and civil with his response.

In stunned silence, I studied him, almost too afraid to ask my next question. He had a sense of nobility about him, but at the same time, I feared him. "I'd like to know one more thing..."

He continued to avoid eye contact to prevent anymore awkwardness. "Not tonight." His attitude settled into cool detachment. "I'm tired and you seem fine to me, so you can let yourself out now. I need to get some rest."

L taught me that cruelty could be so much harsher when it was quiet and contained. I felt an unexpected degree of tension between us. I almost persisted in my inquiries but I decided to hold my tongue.

As badly as I wanted to ask him about the guns, I took that as my cue to leave. *One thing Ms. Alaïa Westbrook never does is wear her welcome out.* I'd just have to get my answers some other time and some other way.

24

CHLOÈ

My gladiator sandal heels clicked against the wooden planks as I walked over to my fiancée. Ahmad was handsome that day in a linen shirt, khaki cargo shorts, and Polo boat shoes. He stood at the edge of the dock near a beautiful yacht resting on *Castaic Lake*.

I should've known better than to wear heels, but I wanted to make his head turn. If I had to sacrifice comfortability, then so be it. I was determined to make him proud to call me his wife.

Throughout life, my mother instilled in me the belief that a lady was always supposed to present herself as such. My hair should always be done, my nails should always be painted, and I should always be in a pair of 6-inch heels, nothing less. Since childhood, my mother had practically drilled perfection into me.

Wearing an ivory sundress, I looked immaculate that afternoon. My hair was down, and Chanel sunglasses covered my light brown eyes. My makeup was minimal. I knew we'd be out all day, and I didn't want to melt in the sun.

"How'd you know I was the outdoorsy type," I asked once I reached him.

Ahmad turned towards me and smiled, making my heart flutter in my chest. "I just had a feeling," he said.

From the pier, I admired the luxury three-tier vessel. It was the perfect escape from the city—which even I needed a break from every now and then. "This is beautiful."

"The best for the best," he said, handing me the keys to it. "And it's yours."

"Ahmad, you can't be serious," I laughed. "I don't even know to drive one of these things."

"You my woman. You don't have to worry about doing anything. I'll handle it."

I smiled, loving the way he pampered me. "A girl can't argue with that."

Ahmad mounted the yacht, and then offered his hand to help me on board. Taking in the breathtaking scenery, I admired the bluish green waters, and the way the sun sparkled against it. It was absolutely vibrant.

"Hey, you hungry?" he asked.

"Hungry is an understatement." Just the thought of some food caused my stomach to grumble. I'd only eaten a power bar earlier, and it was well past lunch time.

"I hope you like seafood," he said.

"Ironically, it's my favorite."

"Well, that's music to my ears," he smiled.

Taking me by the hand, Ahmad led me to the third-tier, where a table full of seafood dishes awaited us. Fresh-caught lobster, softshell crab, fried oyster and shrimp, and Cajun crawfish had my mouth watering uncontrollably.

"Oh my God. You made all this?" I asked in astonishment.

He chuckled. "I had a lil' help."

"This looks so good, I wanna kiss the chef."

Ahmad laughed and led the way. Pulling out a seat for me, he made my plate and poured me a glass of wine. He was so nurturing and sweet. I couldn't see him harming a fly, and I couldn't, for the life of me, figure out why Miracle found him so suspicious.

That bitch was just hating. She just wishes she had a real one.

I'd been hoeing around that bitch for years, and she never once passed judgment on any of the tricks I dated. But now that I'd found a decent man, she just had to try and discourage me. If it were her, I'd be all for it, but since it wasn't, she was salty.

Oh well. Fuck 'em. This is my life to live, and

I'mma live it how I want to.

Ahmad took a seat and made himself a plate. "So, have you thought more about the wedding date?" he asked.

We hadn't discussed the details since the night that I accepted his proposal. He left it all up to me, and he would simply cover the cost for everything. I could have it anywhere I wanted, and in any theme that I desired. With the type of paper Ahmad was making, the possibilities were endless.

"I was thinking we could have a summer ceremony. Gives me some time to tell my friends and family."

He raised an eyebrow, curiously. "You haven't told them yet?" His tone was a mixture of shock and disappointment. He probably thought I updated my Facebook relationship status and everything. It hurt me to know that I'd let him down.

"Not yet. I mean, imagine their reaction after finding out we've only known each other two weeks. I need time to prepare for that level of criticism."

"Well, as your future husband, I'm prepared to endure that storm with you."

His words touched my heart. Every day that we spent together, he made me more and more confident in this crazy ass decision to marry him. My girls would flip once they found out—especially Miracle. She already didn't trust Ahmad...and for unknown reasons.

Looking over at him, I admired his warm spirit and every sexy little thing about him that made him who he was. His curly hair, the faint wrinkles around his green eyes, and his beautiful, heart-stopping smile. Ahmad was the very essence of perfection.

But like they say, if something seems too good to be true, it probably is...

25

CLAIRE

Running a paddle brush over the wigged mannequin head, I thought about the ultimate sacrifice I'd made to get to where I am today. It wasn't just Chloè whose life I'd ruined with my need to stay on top. My twin sister was the first one caught in the crosshairs of my greedy and selfish ways.

Truth be told, it was Cathie who started off as Bruce's side chick. He loved her ass so much that he'd do practically anything for her. I admired how he spoiled her, and showered her in endless luxuries, and I knew immediately that I wanted that lifestyle.

Secretly, I'd always been jealous of my sister. We were identical, but boys had always favored her over me. Perhaps, it was her warm personality that made her more magnetic. Either way, she'd always had more success catching the attention of a rich nigga. Lucky for me, that rich nigga just so happened to be Bruce Hanley.

I fell in love with him at first sight, and was hell-bent on having him. Jealousy eventually overpowered rationality, and I killed my sister just to have him for myself, staging her death to look like an overdose.

Stealing my sister's identity, I continued to live a life, pretending to be her—which included raising her two-year old daughter, Chloè. In the beginning, I just wanted my sister's man, but overtime I grew addicted to the fast life and fast money.

When Chloè became of age, I started pimping her out to Hollywood A-listers, rappers, and anyone that would pay to have my daughter on his arm. Sometimes I felt remorseful for what I was putting her through. But the love of cold hard cash made all of my guilt dissipate. At the end of the day, these niggas were only good for one thing.

All of a sudden, my phone started ringing. As promised, Ahmad hit me right after his date with my daughter. "Whaddup? What'chu into? You fucking with a nigga tonight or what?"

He'd been ignoring my calls these last few days, so I really wasn't feeling his ass right now. "Oh, so now you fucking with a bitch today. I swear, you so mothafucking bipolar. I don't know why the fuck you fronting. You know this pussy got yo mind. That's why the fuck you on this line right now."

"Oh, you talking like you ready for me to come beat that shit up. Don't talk me to death. You betta be 'bout that life when it's time for me to blow down on yo ass."

"I been 'bout that life, nigga. Don't forget I'm the master-mind behind this shit."

"Aight, master mind. I'm 'bout to come put this shit on yo ass."

My pussy started tingling as he talked that arrogant talk. The nigga was 20 years younger than me, but had my mothafucking head gone. Not only did Ahmad have the looks, money, and status. He also had a swagger to match. One that was incomparable.

"You know we gotta get a room...'cuz Chloe will be back soon."

"You know that shit already handled."

"And don't think you gon' bring no hoes in this shit, nigga. This us," I told him.

Ahmad chuckled. "Now you *know* I got enough dick to give the both of ya'll."

"Well, it's good you got enough money to handle the both of us too."

26

MIRACLE

Puffing on a blunt, I watched as my brothers loaded shotguns, assault rifles, and handguns. It was only supposed to be a simple kidnapping and ransom, but these niggas were gearing up like they were ready for war.

We were all in the basement of my grand mama's home. Now that she was blind with debilitating health, they used her crib to trap out of. Mommy was probably rolling over in her grave, but it is what it is. At the end of the day, we were just trying to get it how we lived—even at the cost of loyalty.

"Remember...don't hurt her unless we have to. She may be a lick, but she's still my girl. I don't want her to end up dead," I told Marlon and MiKel.

"Her fate was sealed the moment you agreed to this shit. So, don't front like you ain't know the penalty for pulling a lick."

Nerves on edge, I took another pull. I was battling emotions within myself. I knew the cost that came with robbing my girl, but suddenly my guilt was flaring up. I mean, Alaïa was my best friend. She may've been arrogant, self-centered, and dim-witted, but she was the closest thing that I had to a sister. She was like family to me.

Setting her up would be foul, but my brothers had a point. If she loved me like she said she did, she would've put me on a long time ago. Instead, she let me be her lackey for years, staying in her shadow while she lived life glamorously in the spotlight. Everything she had, she owned. Meanwhile, I was still renting. Even though I made good money, it wasn't enough to equate for all of the time and hard work that I dedicated to her career. If I knocked her ass off top, then I'd have my shot at stealing her fame.

It would finally be my time to shine. It wasn't like I didn't already know the ins-and-outs of the entertainment industry. I could represent my damn self. My brothers had stated facts. Holding onto that bitch like life support wouldn't get my ass nowhere in life. I had to sever the ties if I wanted to soar high.

Alaïa ain't been doing shit but holding me back.

"You already came this far," MiKel said. "Ain't no sense in bitching out now."

He wasn't lying. I'd done most of the legwork by telling her she got the role of "Cameron". Her dumb ass really didn't. I just fed her that lie as an excuse to get her alone. Ever the excellent liar, I played the role of a con with ease, acting my part to the hilt. After all, I was a starving Hollywood actress. It was nothing to pull that lie out of my ass.

Alaïa was under the impression that we were going to celebrate. But the only thing I was celebrating was her mothafucking downfall.

"You right. Fuck it. Let's do this shit."

27

L

The following afternoon, I bumped into Alaïa, who was leaving out at the same time as me. She was dressed in a crop top, jeans, and knee-high boots. A stark contrast to my gym attire and boxing gloves tossed casually over my shoulder. Despite the many bruises on her face, she was beautiful beyond comparison.

Before we had the chance to speak, her phone started ringing. "What does Miracle want?" she asked herself. "Oh yeah. I almost forgot about our little celebration. Completely slipped my mind."

"Talking to yourself like a crazy person," I said. "Like we don't have enough of those in LA."

Alaïa put her phone down and glared at me suspiciously. I could see the thoughts running through her head without her uttering a single word; there was obviously something she was burning to ask. "Where you on yo way to?" she asked, sidling up beside me. As usual, she ignored my brusque demeanor, and took that as her cue to start fucking with me.

"Where does it look like I'm on my way to?" I said gruffly. "It's a shame how fine you are with no mothafucking sense." I shook my head in disappointment.

"So you *do* think I'm fine?" she teased. "Even with all these bumps and bruises?"

The fact that I called her stupid completely went over her head. "If you stopped running that mouth all the time and started learning how to defend yourself, you wouldn't have all them bumps and bruises." The light insult covered my soft undertone and the fact that I really cared about her.

"Then teach me how to," she said. "All my life I've gone without knowing how to fight. I wanna be able to protect myself in case some shit like that ever happens again. Please let me tag along. I promise you, I'm a fast learner," she said with an anticipatory smile.

I fixed a disapproving look on her. "Fine. Go change your shit. I ain't got all day."

She smiled and ran off to change into some workout clothes, totally undaunted by my lack of enthusiasm. After sliding into some yoga pants and a sports bra, she rushed back out and found me already on the elevator. She had to put her arm between the doors just to keep them from closing on her. I was really about to leave her ass too.

"Your ass better practice some patience."

"Nah. Yo ass better practice punctuality," I said in petty triumph.

I swear, between the two of us, we had enough pride to make a third person.

Downstairs, valet fetched my Audi R8, and together we climbed in and headed towards Santa Monica. Half an hour later, we arrived at my empty boxing gym, located a few blocks from the beach. As we pulled into the lot, I told her that I purchased it last year. I explained that it was still being renovated, and once the upgrades were complete, I planned to open it to the public.

As I spoke, I noticed that Alaïa seemed to hang onto every word that I said. She listened with intent, and never once interrupted. It was a total 180 from when we first met back at the club. Slowly but surely, I was cracking her mask to reveal the humanity underneath.

Leading the way to the building, Alaïa followed me inside. Despite its current construction, the place looked nice and like a good investment. There were natural wood-finished floors throughout, warehouse windows, black punching bags, and a boxing ring in the center of the room. Plastered on every wall was a poster of a legendary boxer. Henry Armstrong, Rocky Marciano, Mike Tyson, Muhammad Ali, and Joe Louis. It would be every young fighter's home away from home.

"You gon' teach me how to bite someone's ear off?" Alaïa teased.

Without showing the slightest inkling of amusement, I grabbing my gloves and slung them in her direction, bopping her in that mouth of hers. "Boxing ain't about shit-talking. It's about showing strategy," I said. "Get them gloves on and meet me in the ring."

I pulled on a pair of worn out gloves and joined her. "Starting out, you wanna have a proper boxing stance, and be ready to attack or defend at all times. Your dominant hand and foot should be in back and your knees slightly bent." I demonstrated by showing my stance. "Your weight should be evenly distributed across both legs. Feet diagonal, elbows up, head behind your gloves. You try."

I had to come behind her to help her a few times. Every time that I touched her, I was reminded that it was only a matter of time before my real feelings came pushing to the surface.

Alaïa was beautiful, funny, and willful. I fronted like she wasn't my type, yet I felt our emotional connection on a gut level. She was a constant presence that I'd come to depend on. Alaïa was the very epitome of what I craved. She had my heart, but risking everything for love seemed like a foolish gamble.

It was a mangled way of thinking, but it was how I managed to survive. Pushing those thoughts to the back of my mind, I showed her some basic combat and self-defense moves. I taught her about footwork, pivoting, and counter-attacks. What started out as an innocent course soon turned into something else.

Alaïa smiled. "*Ahh*. Look at those eyes. Now *you're* the one looking at *me* in some kind of way."

"Well...you know what they say. The eyes don't lie."

Before my words could resonate, I bent down and gave her a kiss. Hoisting her up, she wrapped her arms around my neck. Her mouth roughly and possessively crushed against mine, and it felt like her kiss would take my breath away.

Backing her up into the corner of the ring, we began removing each other's clothes at a frenzied pace. Her pants, my shirt, her bra, my sweats. All of our clothes fell onto the floor in a heap as I picked her up and placed her on the top rope.

Grabbing her breasts, I fondled them, pinching delicately on her nipples. Her breasts were surprisingly large, maybe a full 36C, and they looked amazing with her long, lean frame. She had a small patch of brown pubic hair, which was a striking contrast to her freshly shaven pussy lips.

She kissed me passionately as I felt her nipples slide through each of my fingers. They became instantly erect, causing her to release a deep, guttural moan. Sliding my hand along her smooth, brown thigh, I dipped two of my fingers inside her honey pot. Alaïa spread her legs slightly, allowing me to caress her juicy pussy. My body pressed against hers, pushing my pelvis against her leg, so she could feel all 12-inches of this meat.

She wasn't the sweet image I'd built up in my head. Alaïa was a freak.

She kissed down my jawline and started moaning in my ear. My other hand went to the back of her head as I placed a trail of kisses down her neck, biting playfully on the way. As I teased her unmercifully, my fingers continued to thrust in and out of her.

She moved her hand down my body, gripping my thick, meaty dick. In a slow, rhythmic pace, she began to slide her hand up and down my length. She started breathing harder, like she was getting her thrills from jacking me off. Perhaps, my size and girth excited her.

Lowering myself at waist level, I spread her legs and dipped my head between them. A tiny moan escaped as I touched her pussy with my mouth, sliding my tongue between its dewy folds. It was tentative at first, but the sweet, slippery taste of her made me want to press on. Stretching out my tongue as far as it could go, I licked her glistening slit from the bottom to the very top, not neglecting to tickle the clit.

Alaïa moaned and squirmed as I slowly circled her clit and sucked it delicately. I slid my tongue back inside her, wriggling it around while my teeth lightly nibbled at her wet pussy. Her sounds turned me on and made me feel more aggressive. I started sucking on her clit harder, stroking my dick as I drove my tongue deep inside her.

I could feel her shifting her body around, and when I looked up to see what she was doing, she had both of her feet propped up on opposite ropes. Her legs were spread wide as she further opened herself up to me.

I took that opportunity to lick her tight little asshole.

Alaïa spread her pussy lips for me, and I slurped and licked at it for all it was worth. All of my inhibitions were being forced out of me as I displayed all of my passion.

I slid my tongue over her fingers as she began moving them, rubbing herself. I licked away at her fingers and pussy as we both slid up and down her open slit. Dropping lower, I tongued her hole again. In and out I went, wiggling my tongue as I lapped at her insides.

"Cum on my tongue," I whispered. "Do it. Cum for me, baby."

Alaïa started grinding her hips against my face, in rhythm with my tongue, her breathing raging and uncontrolled. She watched as I sucked on her juicy pussy, not stopping till I felt her body tense up and her legs start to tremble.

Alaïa came all on my face and beard, and I greedily licked up every drop of her womanly essence. Standing to my feet, I wiped my wet mouth. Alaïa was still dazed from her climax as I nudged the tip of my dick at her opening, threatening to split her in half. She was so damn tight that I almost gave up on stuffing it inside.

Her tits jiggled sexily as she fought to accept every inch. "Damn, L. Oh my God," she sighed.

"All that shit you be talking, girl, you know you can take this dick."

I sucked on her thick, pouty lips as I sunk half my dick in her. Four thrusts and I was in there, stroking her insides with 12 inches of steel. Grabbing her ass, I rammed into her pussy, in and out, at an even speed. Her tight, warm walls gripped my dick like a glove.

Alaïa creamed all over my shaft, and the sight of it turned me on. Spreading her ass even wider, I plunged deeper, fucking her like my body knew no fatigue. Alaïa took the dick like a pro, thrusting her hips forward to catch every stroke.

I sucked and plucked at her nipples as I felt my climax build up. Two more strokes were all it took to start shooting off like an Uzi in her womb.

Lifting her in my arms, I carried her over towards the center of the ring and placed her down, our bodies never once disconnecting. With a determined look on my face, I started fucking her slowly in missionary.

"Oh, shit, L," she moaned. "Fuck me."

My abdomen flexed every time I pumped into her. I fucked her hard, passionately, and until her pussy muscles started contracting. It was a wondrous feeling to finally have my way with her feisty ass, and I was determined to give her body everything it had been missing.

On the brink of cumming, her toes curled and her eyes slammed shut. I nibbled on her chin as her mouth fell open in ecstasy. I plunged in that pussy like a plumber till she rocked with a violent spasm that curled her toes. "I'm cumming!" she bellowed.

"That's it, baby. Cum for me."

I kissed her neck and shoulder as my dick erupted for the second time. I should've been strapped up, but we were too far gone to think rationally. Rolling over onto the mat, I drew her close to me and held her.

"How'd you get this scar on your nose?" she asked suddenly.

Assailed by painful memories, I looked away, unwilling to satisfy her curiosity.

Alaïa surprised me when she kissed my scar. "You don't have to be so guarded," she said. "I wanna know everything there is to know about you...even the things you may think I don't want to know."

I wanted to say something to put her mind at ease, but I was woefully unequipped with such social skills. So instead, I pulled her close, smiled at her with adulation, and kissed her forehead. For once, my hard exterior slipped a little. Overridden by her insistence, I was slowly letting her in. Alaïa was seeing all my layers beneath the wickedness and evilry.

"You act so cold and like a bad boy...but in reality, you're warm and kind," she said. She was attentive by nature.

A kindred spirit that understood me more than I had anticipated. However, I was certain that her sentiments would change if she knew the truth about me. If it were up to me, she'd never find out. I wanted to hold onto this feeling of peace forever. It was the first time that I actually felt normal.

After an encore in the shower, we left the boxing gym tired and exhausted. We were just about to hop in the foreign when we heard the sudden sound of a milli cocking back. An ominous feeling suggested that it could've been Zane, but when I turned around, I saw the last person I expected to see.

"Remember me?"

Cornered by the chick I'd framed for Jason's murder, I stared down the barrel of her hammer in defeat.

"L, what the fuck is going on?" Alaïa asked, fearfully. "What the fuck is this?"

"Go ahead, *L*. Tell her what's happening and why it's happening. Tell her who I am and how you left me to take the mothafucking charge." Emotionally battered, she pointed the gun at my head. "YOU CAN'T BEGIN TO IMAGINE EVERYTHING YOU COST ME!" she screamed. "I lost my scholarship, my freedom! I LOST EVERYTHING! And now, bitch, it's time for *you* to lose every mothafucking thing!"

Alaïa winced at the force of her words. I was too prideful to even fake like I was remorseful...because truthfully, I wasn't. The only reason I was showing any type of concern was to keep her from harming Alaïa. Once again, I'd taken on the never-ending role as her protector.

"In two weeks, I'll be sentenced," she said. "But I'll go happily knowing that you're going down with me."

Just seeing her there threw my insides into turmoil. Never in a million years, did I see this shit coming. It never dawned on me that someone was tailing me, waiting for the opportunity to strike. As cautious and careful as I usually was, I had somehow gotten caught up in this shit.

In a lost, bitter state of mind, I thought back to our tussle in Jason's room and how she knocked off my mask. I should've never let that bitch live once she'd seen my face.

"Listen. Shit ain't gotta be this way. I know you're angry...You have every right to be...but this shit ain't got nothin' to do with Alaïa. Just let her walk...Take your problems out on me."

She eyed me with cold contempt. "Mothafucka, you not in the position to negotiate! And quite frankly, I don't give a fuck about this nasty ass bitch. Matter fact—"

POP!

Without warning, she shot Alaïa in the chest at point blank range.

I barely had a second to react before I charged at her full-speed.

POP!

POP!

Two bullets to the mid-section stopped me in my tracks.

TO BE CONTINUED

JADED PUBLICATIONS Presents

BAD & Boujee 2

SASHA DAVENPORT

24178101R00099

Printed in Great Britain
by Amazon